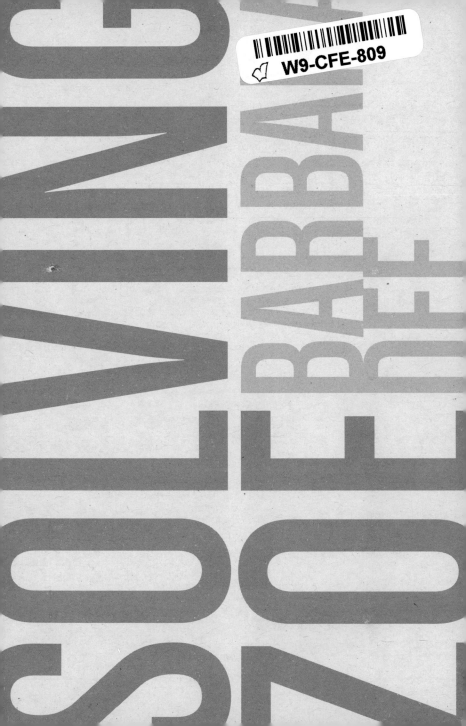

# SOLVING ZOE

**BARBARA DEE**

SCHOLASTIC INC.

New York Toronto London Auckland
Sydney Mexico City New Delhi Hong Kong

# TO MY MOM AND DAD

No part of this publication may be reproduced, stored in a retrieval system, or transmitted in any form or by any means, electronic, mechanical, photocopying, recording, or otherwise, without written permission of the publisher. For information regarding permission, write to Margaret K. McElderry Books, an imprint of Simon & Schuster Children's Publishing Division, 1230 Avenue of the Americas, New York, NY 10020.

ISBN 978-0-545-23793-2

12 11 10 9 8 7 6 5 4 3 2 1          10 11 12 13 14 15/0

Printed in the U.S.A.                                    40

First Scholastic printing, January 2010

Book design by Michael McCartney
The text for this book is set in Vendetta.

# ACKNOWLEDGMENTS

Warmest thanks to my wonderful editor, Karen Wojtyla, and to my fabulous agent, Jill Grinberg. Thanks also to Denise Shannon for her generosity and encouragement, and to Sarah Payne for all her help.

All my love and gratitude to Alex, Josh, and Lizzy, and especially, as always, to my husband, Chris. I couldn't do it without you.

At first Zoe didn't notice that the boy at the end of the table was writing down every word she said.

She barely noticed him at all, the way his blond hair flopped into his face as he sat hunched over what looked like a small notebook. Probably he was just some applicant taking notes about the lunchroom: "Burgers at the Lorna Hubbard School extremely gross," or something brilliant like that.

And anyway, why would Zoe pay attention to some kid she didn't even know, when she was finally, after an endless morning, getting to see her best friend, Dara Grosbard? The only class they had together this year was gym, and that didn't even count, because you had to spend the whole time dodging basketballs or jogging breathlessly around the track. So the one place they could talk was the ear-splitting Hubbard lunchroom, where you really had to concentrate to have a meaningful conversation.

"God, Zoe, this is absolutely disgusting," Dara was

saying as she chomped on a chili dog. "You sure you don't want a bite?"

"Positive," Zoe answered. She opened her bag of Lay's potato chips and dumped them onto her tray. Usually there were twelve chips per bag; if she did it just right, she could fit all twelve into her tuna fish sandwich. For crunch, she used to explain to horrified onlookers. Of course, by now everybody knew all about Zoe's sandwich weirdness and didn't even ask.

"So how was Chinese today?" Zoe said, poking in the last of her chips. "Did he make you talk?"

"He always makes us talk. I should have taken a normal language, like French."

"French? You think French is *normal*?"

"Okay, maybe not," Dara agreed. "But if I took French, at least we'd be together for one measly class besides gym. Sigh."

Zoe smiled. Dara was always saying things like "sigh" and "gasp," as if she were attaching smiley faces, or frownies, to all her sentences. But at least that way you knew what she was feeling, Zoe thought as she took a crunchy bite of sandwich, then a cooling sip of chocolate milk.

Suddenly she felt a light poke from behind.

"Are these seats taken?"

She turned her head. Surprisingly, it was Allegra Hillenbrand, who insisted on being called Leg, along with her bodyguard, Paloma Farrelly. They were both really good dancers, two of the best in Hubbard Middle Division.

"No, they're free," Dara was saying nicely. "If you can squeeze in."

Zoe gave Dara a look that meant, *Do we have to?* But either Dara didn't notice or else she didn't think she had a choice. She pushed aside her chili dog and slid over to make room, so that Leg and Paloma wouldn't have to sit too close to the unknown boy with the notebook.

Leg smiled at Dara. "So," she said. "Have you officially signed up yet?"

"Signed up for what?" Zoe asked. Out of the corner of her eye she could see the boy turn a page in his notebook and write something quickly.

"Nothing," Dara said. "It's stupid, Zoe."

"No, it's not. It's brilliant," Leg insisted.

Zoe glanced at Dara. "What is?"

"Nothing," Dara said again. Her gray-blue eyes narrowed in embarrassment. "Leg thinks I should try out for the musical."

"The musical?" Zoe said. "You *want* to?"

"I'm not sure." Dara nibbled on her thumbnail. "Maybe."

"Oh, you're totally sure, Dara," Leg said. "You said so right before Chinese." She flipped her shiny chestnut hair over one shoulder, her gold hoop earrings catching the light. "Besides, why go to an amazing school like Hubbard if you don't take advantage, blah blah blah. You should encourage her, Zoe."

"*Do* you want to?" Zoe repeated, trying to ignore Leg. "Because nobody should force you, Dara."

"Nobody is," said Paloma.

"Sigh," Dara said. "The thing is, Zoe, I think I might want to try out, but I'm terrified. You know what Izzy always says."

Zoe nodded. Zoe's sixteen-year-old sister, Isadora, was the star of almost every Hubbard production, but even she always complained about tryouts. She called them *cutthroat,* and how could they not be, really, with all the gifted and talented kids strutting around this "amazing" school? And the thing was, Dara was shy—talented but shy. And also tiny: not the best combination, especially when you were expected to stand onstage and sing into a blaring microphone.

*Poor Dara,* Zoe thought. *She doesn't know what she's in for.*

Paloma laughed. "Well, look at it this way, Dara. You probably won't even get a part, so there's nothing to worry about, right?"

"You shouldn't say that," Zoe said, her dark eyes flashing. "Dara's actually an incredible singer. If she wants a part, she'll get one."

"Well, yeah, Zoe. Obviously."

"So if it's obvious, Paloma, you shouldn't tease her like that."

"It was just a joke," Dara said gently. "Never mind, Zoe."

Zoe realized then that all three girls were looking at her, and Paloma was smiling. She felt like a complete moron, all of a sudden.

"Okay, then," Leg said finally. "I guess our work here is done. See you later, Dara." Then she and Paloma walked away, taking dramatic turned-out steps, as if to remind everyone in the lunchroom that they were both really good dancers.

Zoe took a small bite of her tuna-and-potato-chip sandwich. "You want me to come with you to tryouts?" she asked.

"Oh, definitely *not*," Dara said. "You hate all that stuff, Zoe. It would make you crazy to sit there. Besides, we'd probably just look at each other and start laughing hysterically." She reached over and took a sip of Zoe's chocolate milk. "I'll just meet you afterward, okay? If you don't mind waiting a tiny bit."

"Of course I don't mind," Zoe said, surprised this was even a question. "Why would I?" Suddenly she remembered something. "I've got Isaac's after school today. I really can't be late."

"Oh, you won't be," Dara promised. "I'll be like ten or fifteen minutes."

*Well, ten or fifteen minutes probably won't make much of a difference*, Zoe thought. And even if Dara refused to come inside, they'd have the walk over together. And of course they'd have the walk back to Zoe's.

"Okay, great," she said cheerfully. "I'll meet you in the lobby."

And then a strange thing happened. The blond floppy-haired boy at the end of the table looked right into Zoe's eyes, the very second she finished speaking. Then he stuffed his notebook into his pocket and walked rapidly out of the cafeteria.

And Zoe couldn't say why, but she knew right then that he'd been eavesdropping on the entire conversation. And possibly worse than that: possibly writing it all down in that little spiral notebook, although of course at that point she didn't have any proof.

# 2

Leg was right: Hubbard really was an amazing place. And Zoe Bennett knew perfectly well that she didn't deserve to be there.

Her sister, Isadora, deserved to be there. So did her ninth-grade brother, Malcolm, who was a jerk half the time, but also a genius in math.

The school was perfect for them: a sprawling expanded brick mansion once belonging to some famous Brooklyn socialite, where superstar kids could study Robotics and African Drumming, and never have to deal with grades or report cards or bells or red pens. Even the teachers were amazing—published authors, semi-famous artists, and fresh-out-of-excellent-college types with nose rings and blue hair. You called them all by their first names. *They were like friends,* Zoe often thought, *except in reality.*

Lunch was over, and Zoe was in Math class. She watched her Math teacher, Anya, write three Do Nows on the whiteboard, the way she always did at the start of class. Anya was maybe the coolest-looking teacher at Hubbard, with a blue-black raptor tattoo on her left bicep, and a big red Pegasus on her left calf. But for all her coolness, she still had bossy rules, like always making you "show your work," even if the answer was completely obvious. And by the time Zoe had copied down the three Do Nows each day and pretended to "show work" she'd never even done, her brain would be flying in all directions at once, like one of those swirl paintings you make in neighborhood street fairs. She'd start doodling in her Math notebook, and then she'd have some fascinating thought, and the next thing she'd know, the period would be over and she wouldn't have finished the second Do Now.

This was Zoe's latest fascinating thought: Every number was actually a color. Not in some silly random paint-by-number way, but in a real way that made its own sense. Zoe wasn't in charge of that sense; she didn't wake up one morning and decide, *Today I'll assign colors to the first nine digits, tra-la-la.* She just gradually realized that whenever she thought of the number four, her mind would be bathed in a beautiful sky blue. And whenever she considered the number five, she'd see a deep vivid emerald green. Pretty soon she had a whole rainbow of numbers worked out in her head:

1 = *White*

2 = *Light blue*

3 = *Red*

4 = *Beautiful sky blue*

5 = *Deep vivid emerald green*

6 = *Orange*

7 = *Yellow (Bright yellow, not sick yellow)*

8 = *Purple*

9 = *Chocolate Brown*

She didn't have it all worked out yet; she didn't know, for example, what happened when you got to ten. But for now she was happy just doodling with the few Prismacolor pencil stubs she'd secretly fished out from the bottom of her backpack: first a red tornado (all angry spirally 3s), then a beautiful sky blue sailboat (the sail obviously a 4), then a bunch of purple clouds (big gentle billowy 8s). Doodling-by-numbers was lots of fun, a painless way to get through Anya's boring class.

Two nights ago at dinner, Zoe had casually mentioned the number-color theory to her family. That had been a mistake.

"I don't get it, Zoe," Malcolm had said. "You mean if I say a number, some *color* pops into your head?"

"Well, yes."

"So, what pops into your head if I say two thirds? Or negative three trillion? Or 3.14159?"

"Oh, Malcolm," said Isadora. "Will you please just give her a break?"

"No, no, I'm really wondering."

"I don't see numbers with decimals," Zoe explained patiently. "I'm talking about ordinary digits. One through nine."

Malcolm snorted. "But you can't limit it to the first nine digits. That makes no mathematical sense."

"Why not?" asked Dad, winking at Zoe.

"Because if you say something like, okay, three equals pink—"

"It doesn't," Zoe said. "Three is red."

"Whatever. Then when you perform any operation on three—"

"I'm not a doctor, Malcolm!"

"I mean a *mathematical* operation. When you combine it with another number, you're changing the value in a way that can't possibly correspond to your whole color theory, right?"

Zoe put down her fork. "I don't understand a word you're talking about, Malcolm. All I said was—"

"I know, I know. Two equals blue."

"*Light* blue. Four is *sky* blue."

"Isn't sky blue the same as light blue?" Isadora wondered.

"Oh no," Zoe said quickly. "Sky blue is pure blue, like if you close your eyes and think of the word *blue*. Two is sort of a pale aquamarine. It's totally different."

"Blue is my best color," Spencer announced. He was three years old, and he didn't even have his colors straight. "I want ketchup."

"Please," prompted Mom.

"Pleasepleaseplease."

"I'll re-explain my point," said Malcolm, gesturing with his fork.

"Actually, Malcolm, you're completely *missing* the point," Zoe said, her voice starting to squeak a bit. "All I meant—"

"Was that numbers equal colors. Yeah, I know."

"Malcolm, watch that tone," warned Mom. "It's bordering on hostile. And Zoe, calm down, get your hair away from your food, and eat your salad."

Isadora made a face. "Speaking of salad," she said to Mom, "did you buy a different kind of ranch dressing? This one tastes funny."

"It's lower fat," Mom said, examining the label. "I think it tastes fine."

Dad cleared his throat. "Getting back to Zoe's number theory," he said meaningfully. Malcolm made another snorting sound.

Zoe could feel her cheeks burn. "Never mind, Dad. It's not important. Can we please just drop it?"

"Why should we? Your theory's really interesting, Zozo. Maybe not in a mathematical way, but in an artistic way."

Dad was an artist. He was always saying things like that, trying to make Zoe feel creative.

"I wonder," he continued, "how Zoe would react to different color combinations. Or to patterns of colors. Would she see them as numbers? And would she be more likely to see numbers in an abstract painting?"

"What difference does it make?" grunted Malcolm, balling up his napkin. "This whole topic is completely brain-dead."

Mom put down the salad dressing. "Excuse me, Malcolm, but I never want to hear that word again. It's highly offensive."

"Okay, sorry. It's completely *illogical*, then. Better, Mom?"

"Slightly."

Dad glanced at Zoe, but she was staring intently at her

plate, not caring that her long, curly hair was tumbling into her face. "Anyway," he said to Malcolm in an aren't-we-having-fun sort of voice, "what's so great about logic? Who says Zoe has to be logical?"

"She's talking about numbers, Dad! Numbers are supposed to be logical! That's what they're for!"

Mom frowned. "Do we really have to have a raging debate about this at the supper table? Can't we please just have a pleasant conversation after a long, hard day?" She was an orthodontist; sometimes her patients were, as she put it, "a little bit resistant." Apparently this had been one of those days.

"And what about zero?" Malcolm demanded. "Don't tell me zero has a color!"

Zoe sighed. "It doesn't, Malcolm. I never said it did."

"Zerozerozero," sang Spencer. "I have zero ketchup left!"

Suddenly everyone looked at the youngest Bennett. Spencer had ketchup on his cheeks, the tip of his nose, both hands, and down the front of his shirt. He looked alarmingly like a stunt toddler in a slasher movie.

"Oh, Spence," Mom groaned. "What a mess. Why did you do that?"

"Zero is red," he sang. "Red on my head." He used his ketchupy fingers to give himself a shampoo. Then he began clapping for himself, sending little squirts of ketchup in all directions.

That had ended the conversation, and for Zoe not a moment too soon. Why had she even tried sharing her theory with her family? If what she said wasn't intellectually perfect or artistically significant, if it didn't star Isadora or Spencer, or stand up to Malcolm's penetrating mathematical analysis, then naturally the Bennetts wouldn't understand. Well, it didn't matter that much, anyway. She'd talk about her theory with Dara. Maybe she'd tell it to her this afternoon, after that pointless tryout for the musical. Dara would think it was fascinating, even if nobody else did.

"So I guess that's it," Anya was saying brightly. *Oh, right: Math class. Do now!* "Zoe? Any thoughts?"

"Not really." Zoe could feel her cheeks start to redden. *Three.*

"Oh, come on," Anya was coaxing her, as if Zoe were at her first ever swimming lesson and refused to wet her big toe. "Join the conversation! Don't be afraid."

"I'm not afraid."

Paloma turned around and grinned at her just the way she had at lunch. And then Mackenzie Stafford, who went around telling everybody that she had "a near-photographic memory," began giggling.

"That's great, Zoe," Anya said, nodding. "Think of it this way: Numbers are sort of like toys. Try to play with them a little. You know, relax and mess around. Don't worry about being right or wrong. Just have some fun with them, okay?"

And all of a sudden Anya was right by Zoe's desk. She was looking down at Zoe's notebook with a funny expression on her face. "Is this what you've been doing all class?" she asked quietly, pointing a black-nail-polished fingernail at Zoe's number doodles.

"Um," Zoe answered. "Not *all* class."

Anya leaned over Zoe's desk. She studied the doodles for a couple of seconds. "Really cool. But this isn't Art, you know?"

"Sorry."

Anya shook her head. She cupped her hand and said quietly and distinctly in Zoe's ear, "Listen. I hate to say this, Zoe. But unless I start seeing some actual work from you, you could very easily fail this class."

Then she walked back to her whiteboard and began writing some homework problems, the blue-black raptor on her left arm jumping around frantically, as if it had suddenly found itself locked in a tiny birdcage.

# 3

After horrible, endless Math was Recreation Arts, which at Lorna Hubbard was what you were supposed to call Gym. Rec Arts was all the way down in the basement, so when it was finally over, Zoe had to trudge four flights up the central marble staircase to her Ancient Civilizations class. And then she began to run.

Because just down the corridor she spotted the eavesdropping boy from lunch: the blond head, the hunched shoulders. She had to talk to him—she didn't know why, or what she'd even say. *Hi, my name is Zoe, and why were you spying on me at lunch?* sounded friendly, but definitely paranoid. Besides, maybe she'd imagined the whole thing. She still wanted a better look at him, anyway.

Pushing through a bunch of Upper Division kids blocking the door to the digital recording studio, she rushed past an open classroom in which Randy, the Poetry teacher, was bellowing: "WHAT'S POETRY? WHAT ISN'T POETRY? WHO DECIDES?" On his door someone had duct-taped a huge spray-painted banner announcing tryouts for the musical (TODAY—MONDAY!!!), which reminded Zoe about this afternoon. *Poor Dara,* she thought again as she hurried past an empty mirrored dance studio and then the practice room of the Hubbard Non-Western Percussion Ensemble, all the while keeping the boy's floppy blond hair in view.

And then, somehow, she lost sight of him. She'd just blinked, maybe, right at the moment he'd wandered into some classroom. After all, if he was an applicant, he was probably visiting Hubbard to check out the coolest teachers. *Well, don't be fooled by tattoos,* she warned him telepathically. Then she shoved open the door of Ancient Civs and headed immediately for the back wall, taking her usual seat next to Ezra Blecker, a brilliant boy who wore incomprehensible T-shirts and hardly ever spoke to anyone.

"Hi, Ezra," Zoe said, dumping her backpack onto the floor. "What are you reading?"

He held up a thick paperback: *Samurai in Cyberspace: Blue Screen of Doom.*

"Huh," she said politely. "Is it good?"

"I just started it. So far it's pretty standard."

Zoe nodded, even though she didn't have the slightest idea what Ezra's books were like. At the end of the nod she added a smile, but by now Ezra was reading again, and didn't seem to notice.

"You okay, Zoe?" Paloma called out from the front of the classroom.

"Of course I am," Zoe replied. "Why wouldn't I be?"

"I don't know. Because you seemed so out of it in Math."

Leg was in this class too. She stretched her slender, expressive arms, fluttering the floaty sleeves of her magenta-colored top. "So what happened?" she asked, yawning. "Another out-of-Zoe experience?"

Paloma laughed. "Exactly," she answered, looking over her shoulder at the rest of the class.

The classroom door flew open. There was a predictable ten-second pause, during which everyone, even Paloma and Leg, became silent. Then into the room swept Signe Sorenson, Hubbard's legendary teacher of Ancient Civilizations.

"Good morning," she said in her crackly voice, with its faint aroma of somewhere-in-Europe. She was a small round woman, shaped like a crab apple; often she wore animal-print ponchos or wild paisley shawls that only made her look smaller and rounder. Today she had on an enormous moss green cashmere scarf wound twice around her neck, the long tasseled ends dangling down the front of her black wool dress, trembling when she spoke. With her puffy white hair piled on top of her head like a generous dollop of whipped cream, her red plastic eyeglasses, and her high-top sneakers with their NBA logos, she looked like a grandma doll, as dressed by a naughty color-blind preschooler.

But nobody ever giggled when she made her dramatic entrance. The thing about Signe Sorenson was, she was terrifying. At least she was to Zoe.

Zoe couldn't say why. But probably it had to do with all the unsubstantiated rumors about Signe's life: She'd done something heroic, something top secret, maybe a spy mission behind enemy lines during Vietnam, or the Cold War. Whatever it was, it was very intimidating. So last fall, when Zoe finally met the famous teacher at the Welcome to Middle Division Tea, she had a hundred theories and questions buzzing around in her head. And when Signe Sorenson (who for the Tea had draped herself in an enormous peacock blue mohair shawl) came over to greet the Bennetts, she extended a surprisingly large, warm hand to Zoe.

"Another Bennett," she'd said in that crackly voice. "How very delightful."

"This is Zoe," Mom had said, nodding encouragingly at her daughter.

"Zoe," Signe had repeated. "Such a lovely Greek name. Quite ancient, you know. I have always been fascinated by names."

Zoe glanced uncertainly at her dad. What was she supposed to say to this? But he was no help; he just smiled at her.

Signe Sorenson beamed at Mom, but she continued to hold Zoe's hand. "I truly loved teaching Isadora and Malcolm. Such talented, talented children. You must be so proud." Then she turned to Zoe, still trapping her hand, and scrutinized her face as if she were committing it to memory. "So tell me, Zoe Bennett, what is *your* passion?"

Her passion? Nobody had warned her to have a passion! She looked at Dad again, this time frantically, but he just kept smiling at her, probably because he couldn't think of a passion for her to have either. But she had to say something, or else Signe Sorenson would probably end up amputating her hand. So she just blurted out the first thing that came into her head:

"I like pizza."

Signe smiled. "As do I," she said. She leaned toward Zoe as if she were about to confide a valuable secret. "I have a very strong feeling," she added quietly, "that your answer will change dramatically before you leave our Middle Division."

Then she squeezed Zoe's hand and toddled off to greet Mackenzie Stafford, who was standing with her parents beside the Gluten-Free Table. Signe was trapping Mackenzie's hand but Mackenzie didn't seem to mind. She was chattering on and on, probably about her near-photographic memory, and Signe was nodding encouragingly and smiling back.

"Come on, Zozo, let's go steal some brownies," Dad was urging. "I'll race you."

"No, thanks," Zoe murmured. "I don't want anything." That was true. All she wanted right then was to escape the Tea, because she strongly suspected that she had just been given a test, and had failed somehow.

In September she knew she was right. For the first few days of sixth grade, Signe didn't even seem to notice that Zoe was in her class. Once or twice she glanced in Zoe's direction, but it was pretty clear what she was thinking: *I have led a fabulous, mysterious, significant life, and you, Zoe Bennett, like pizza.*

*Oh, well. Maybe you'll change dramatically before you leave Middle Division.*

Zoe ran her fingers over her desktop. Signe's room had special desks she said she'd ordered from some experimental school in Denmark. Really, they were just little whiteboards you were supposed to write on instead of paper. The idea was that you were allowed to take notes, but immediately you had to "internalize" whatever you'd written, because some other kid in the next class could just erase it with a smeary washcloth.

Now Signe was saying something in that crackly voice about "a truly extraordinary new addition to the class." Zoe glanced up from her whiteboard desk. Signe was beaming as she gestured grandly toward some kid at a desk near the windows. "Cryptoanalytic prodigy," she was saying, or something close to that, with a lot of syllables.

Zoe looked.

It was the boy from lunch. The floppy-haired eavesdropper.

So he wasn't an applicant; he was an actual student. And not only was he at Hubbard, he was in *this class*.

"I'm sure you'll all be giving Lucas a very enthusiastic welcome," Signe said, "in the warmest Hubbard tradition. Yes, Jake?"

Jake Greiner, a kid who spoke seven languages fluently and claimed to know curse words in twenty-three, stood up and faced the windows. He bowed majestically at Lucas. "*Willkommen*, prodigy," he intoned. "*Bienvenidos, Benvenuto, Bienvenue, Welkom* ..."

Everyone laughed, even Ezra.

The boy—Lucas—didn't. He stood, gave a stiff little half-wave to nobody in particular, and then sat down again, blushing.

"Ah, Lucas, dear," Signe said. "Aren't you going to thank Jake for that lovely greeting?"

"Yeah, thanks," Lucas mumbled, not looking up.

Zoe shifted uncomfortably in her seat, causing her chair leg to squeak. That was when Lucas noticed she was in the room. He immediately turned away. Zoe thought she saw him write something, but she couldn't get a good look.

"Excuse me, Lucas. You're not supposed to use notebooks in this class," Mackenzie announced. "That's why we have these desks."

"It's all right, Mackenzie," Signe said calmly. "Now why don't we all shift our attention to ancient Egypt?"

Zoe tried again to peek at Lucas, but she couldn't see past Ezra. She sighed as she unzipped her backpack. *Jake is such an incredible jerk*, she thought. Why did he have to show off like that? Why did *everybody* at Hubbard have to show off all the time? It was like this school was one giant stage, and if you didn't want to be under a glaring spotlight with everybody staring at you every minute, you were lost.

Well, Zoe wasn't lost: She had her own fascinating thoughts. And who cared what Malcolm said about them, or Anya, or anybody else. She reached inside her backpack for the special dry erase marker that you had to use on Signe's desks.

In the upper right-hand corner of her desktop, in the smallest, neatest print she could manage, she wrote:

*4 = Blue.*

And she was very careful for the rest of the class not to accidentally smudge it out.

# 4

Almost every single afternoon Zoe and Dara went to Zoe's apartment. Mostly they just locked themselves in Zoe's bedroom and ate Skittles they'd bought on the way home, and laughed about their classmates. Or made up games, like the one they called Which, where you asked each other which was stupider, hip-hop or heavy metal? Or which was grosser, nose hair or toe fungus? *The Zoe and Dara Show*, Zoe's dad called them, teasingly. Of course, now that they hardly saw each other at school, *The Zoe and Dara Show* was the highlight of the entire day.

But this afternoon Zoe was in the school lobby, waiting. And Dara, who was upstairs auditioning, was already twenty-five minutes late.

Zoe sighed as she adjusted her backpack straps, which were creeping into her armpits. She wished she'd brought a book, or an iPod, or something. There was absolutely nothing to do in this boring lobby but stand there staring at the massive oil portrait of Lorna Hubbard, with her amused eyes and her steel gray hair and her ugly mauve dress. MISS LORNA HUBBARD, FOUNDER, read the small gold plaque underneath the painting. *What an incredibly demented name,* Zoe thought. Lorna Hubbard. Lorna Hubbard. Who would give a baby a name like that, anyway? Maybe it sounded better backward: Anrol Drabbuh. Or possibly Lorna Hubbard was an anagram for something: Rolna Bradbuh. Norla Duh Barb. Hula born drab. Our blah brand?

Suddenly Zoe realized that there was someone else in the lobby. Lucas. He was wearing a ridiculously un-kidlike brown tweed overcoat, and he was sitting on the floor, just about a foot away from the interior swinging doors that led to the auditorium. And, as always, he was hunched over his spiral notebook, writing.

It was a stupid place to sit. But Lucas was new. Obviously he didn't realize that any second some kid could come crashing through those doors and smack him in the head with a saxophone or a tennis racket.

"Excuse me," Zoe called out brightly. "Lucas? That's your name, right?"

"Right," he said, not bothering to look up.

"Um, I don't know if you realize this, but those doors swing into the lobby. Somebody could bump into you if you're sitting there."

"Okay, thanks," he replied.

But he didn't move. He just sat there writing. And then sure enough, maybe ten seconds later, the doors banged open, and Tyler Russo and Calliope Pollock, two of the coolest theater-types in the seventh grade, came barreling through, crashing into Lucas and sending him flying through the lobby.

"Omigod," Zoe cried. "Are you all right, Lucas?"

Lucas got up on his knees. He looked as if he were fighting tears. "I'm fine," he said.

"Sorry," Tyler said. "But why were you sitting there, dude?"

"I can sit wherever I want, cretin. I *go* to this school."

"Yeah? Well, good for you," Tyler said, grinning. "But listen, dude, you were kind of asking to get hit. Sitting on the floor like a little gargoyle—"

"Stop it," Calliope squealed, smacking him playfully on the arm. "You're so mean, Tyler. I hate you."

Zoe could feel her own cheeks start to burn. She looked at Lucas. *Get up*, she willed him silently.

Tyler walked over to Lucas and extended his hand. "Hey, come on, bro, don't be mad. I'll help you up, all right?"

But then all of a sudden Lucas scrambled to his feet and awkwardly ran out the front door, like a tangled marionette that was being yanked offstage. Tyler and Calliope looked at each other and burst into laughter.

"Freak," Calliope pronounced, as they walked past Zoe to join some other theater-types hanging out in front of the building. Zoe peered down the block after Lucas, but he was already out of sight. She glanced at her watch. It was already three twenty; where in the world was Dara? And how much longer would Zoe have to stand there, wasting precious after-school time, waiting?

Then she spotted something. At first she wasn't sure, because the lobby was old and dimly lit, and anything tiny and dark you saw out of the corner of your eye could be a dust ball, or someone's lost glove. But she walked quickly to the interior doors where Lucas had first sat down. Then she picked up a little black object.

His spiral notebook. Left behind in the crash.

Without thinking, she opened the cover.

*PERSONAL PROPERTY!!! KEEP OUT!!!*
*I'll know if you read anything.*

"Don't be ridiculous," she said aloud. Then she turned to the second page.

And then to the third.

And the fourth.

And the fifth.

And the thirteenth.

It didn't matter. Any page she turned to was equally impossible to read.

ⱱ abɫH ɫaↄb bɫɹ∞ↄm ∞kbwH. ɹɹabɫ bσ ⱱ mxↄ∽ɔf aHrH, ɹɹbbɫↄ∽ɔf ↄo ɫↄσH?

? ]:†£&* (. ?' ;£)[.o)&)

What could it mean? She flipped through the pages, hoping that somewhere, maybe in the margins, there was a non-nonsensical clue. But there was nothing, just page after page of odd-looking near-letters and mutant symbols and fragmentary shapes. Why was she even looking at it? Lucas's notebook was completely crazy.

She slipped it into the pocket of her purple hoodie sweatjacket. She'd give it back to him tomorrow, she told herself. In a weird way she felt as if she'd failed him just now, and returning his notebook was a small, nice thing she could do.

Even if he was obviously from another planet.

"Zoe?"

She spun around. "Oh, hi, Mackenzie."

"What are you doing here? Waiting for Dara?"

Zoe nodded.

"Well, I saw her upstairs at tryouts. There's a ton of people ahead of her, so she won't be done for a while. Sorry." Mackenzie took out her cell phone and started dialing.

"Actually," said Zoe, not waiting for Mackenzie to finish her call. "There's something I really have to do, and I can't wait around anymore. Tell Dara if you see her, okay?"

Mackenzie waved at Zoe. "Hi, Mom," she shouted into her cell. "I just auditioned, and guess what!"

Zoe waved back. Mackenzie wasn't so bad, really. Although probably there was no such thing as a *near*-photographic memory.

Zoe strapped on her backpack. Then finally she left Hubbard for the day, patting her hoodie pocket once or twice to make sure nothing had fallen out.

# 5

Zoe wasn't making an excuse when she told Mackenzie there was something she had to do right then. There was, and it really couldn't wait.

She had a job. Her first job ever, and it was incredibly important. And fascinating. And also a teeny bit disgusting.

Zoe was a lizard-sitter. For the next week or so, probably, she was being paid five dollars a day to feed thirty-two reptiles, all living in an elegant brownstone not three blocks from Hubbard.

It happened like this: One day Dad came home extra late from a new painting job. He was a muralist; once in a while he painted an important wall, like on a government building or a bank, but most of the time he painted dining rooms or kids' bedrooms. His two most popular walls were The Hills of Tuscany (dining room) and An Enchanted Forest (first-grade girl's bedroom). He painted these so often that he could do them with his eyes shut. Anyway, that's what he said.

But that day his eyes looked wide open and kind of

stunned. "You've got to see this new job of mine, Zozo," he said, shaking his head.

"What's so amazing about it?" she teased him. "They don't want Tuscany, for a change?"

"Just see it. That's all I'm going to tell you. Here's the address. Meet me there after school tomorrow."

She tried to get him to tell her more, but he refused. The next day Zoe easily found the elegant brownstone, and rapped on the door with the bronze knocker. A tall, bony man with a thin, graying ponytail opened the door. At first she thought she must have read the address wrong, but then Dad appeared and hugged her against his big stomach, enveloping her with his familiar turpentiney smell.

"There you are, Zozo," he said, grinning. "This is Isaac Wakefield. Isaac, this is my daughter Zoe. The one I told you about."

"Pleasure," grunted Isaac. He turned his back and gestured for her to follow. They walked past a high-ceilinged parlor on the right filled with massive tangles of wire, almost like giant Brillo pads.

"Isaac's a wire sculptor," Dad said. "Very famous."

"Hogwash," Isaac shouted over his shoulder. Zoe laughed, because it was the first time outside a cartoon that she had ever heard anyone use that expression.

And apparently she wasn't there to see his sculptures. He led them up the narrow stairs to the second floor. "There, there, and there," he said, pointing to three different rooms. Zoe looked at her father questioningly.

"Reptiles," Dad explained, grinning. "Isaac studies them. All different species. Take a look around, Zozo. Don't be afraid."

She followed Isaac from room to room, gaping at the gleaming, orderly glass terrariums filled with iguanas, geckoes, salamanders, skinks, turtles, newts, anoles, and whiptails. (But no snakes, thank goodness!) Each terrarium was its own miniature reptile world, carefully landscaped with rocks and cacti and grasses and weathered branches. And beside each terrarium was a clipboard holding charts with titles such as "Gecko #4: Cricket Consumption," or "Iguana #2: Water." Zoe watched as Isaac stood perfectly still in front of each terrarium, then scribbled something on the charts.

"Got to be precise," he said, still writing. "They look tough, but their ecosystems are actually pretty delicate. And too much food or water can throw everything off."

"Whoa," Zoe whispered to her father. "This is incredible! But what are we doing here?"

Dad smiled. "Isaac's commissioned me to do his bedrooms. He wants me to paint three different lizard habitats."

"Three? I thought lizards just lived in deserts."

"Some do. And some live in woodlands. Also savannas."

"Oh." Zoe watched a tiny yellow-headed gecko nibble a strawberry. She wondered if it tasted sweet to him; or maybe to a gecko this tasted like a pepperoni pizza. How could you even know? "This is way better than Tuscany," she said in Dad's ear. "But I mean, why *lizards*?"

Suddenly Isaac was facing her. "Why *not* lizards?"

She blushed. "I don't know. They're not exactly—" She struggled for a word.

"Cute? Cuddly?" His eyes sparkled mischievously.

"Well, they aren't really pets," she tried to explain tactfully. "I mean, I saw your charts. They don't even have names. They're just like, Salamander #4."

"It's not their job to be cuddly. Or to have cuddly names. Just watch them, kiddo. Try to understand what you're looking at, and try to keep your overheated emotional preteen reactions out of it."

Zoe laughed. This man was nuts, but she liked him for some reason.

And afterward, when they walked home together, Dad

told her that Isaac lived alone (except for his thirty-two lizards). He had six kids (one of them named Willie, a Hubbard first grader) and three ex-wives. But he was worried about his elderly mother in Arizona. He needed to visit her for a little while, and he needed someone to look after his lizards. All you had to do was feed them and write down what they ate. And, also, if you felt so inclined, maybe jot down a few notes about their behavior....

"You mean *me?*" Zoe asked, finally understanding what her father was saying.

"Sure. Why not you, Zozo?"

It sounded as obvious as when Isaac had asked, *Why not lizards?*

"Because, Dad! They're so slimy! And the ones that aren't slimy have these weird spiny things—"

"Who said anything about touching them?"

"Besides," Zoe argued, "what do I know about lizards?"

Dad squeezed her shoulder. "You don't need to know anything, Zoe. You just need to be willing to learn. After all those years at Hubbard, are you so afraid to open up your brain and use it a little?"

She stared at him. He'd never spoken that way to her before. "Of course not," she said, a bit offended.

And so Dad made all the arrangements. Isaac gave her a key and a key chain he'd sculpted out of wire. There was a funny shape dangling on the end of it, which, Zoe realized with pride, was a letter *Z*. And every afternoon immediately after school, or on the weekend, she was to go to Isaac's brownstone, feed the thirty-two reptiles, record what they ate and drank, and then take a few notes if, as Isaac had put it, "the spirit moved her."

It was a little scary at first, especially because it turned out that Dad had another Enchanted Forest job to finish up first, and wouldn't be starting Isaac's lizard rooms for at least a few days. So the first time Zoe went to Isaac's, she made Dara come with her. But Dara was too grossed out after five minutes in the iguana room, and fled downstairs to hang out with the giant Brillo pads until Zoe was finished.

Today was Zoe's second day. She let herself into the brownstone with her special key and carefully fed the lizards exactly the way Isaac had taught her. It was hard to record their food consumption with the kind of precision he expected, but she did her best. "Iguana #2: 3 1/2 crickets," she wrote in her neatest handwriting. Then she tiptoed around the three bedrooms, stopping every once in a while to record her observations:

*Baby golden gecko hid in leaves, but peeked out once I misted. Seems to like mushy bananas—ate 2 tsps.*

*Newt #2 sat on rock. Bobbed head three times and stared.*

*Green anole palish green, but sometimes brown. Or brown-green. (Or maybe it's green-brown. I don't know what you call it.)*

She crossed the last part out, then watched the small-ish lizard carefully explore the walls of the glass terrarium. *Anole,* she repeated to herself. *Anole. Backward that's Elona, which is actually a beautiful name. Is it any different from Lorna? Oh, of course it is; E, not R. Funny how one letter totally changes everything.*

The house was very still, very quiet. Almost like a kind of lizard lab. Or a peaceful reptile paradise. Suddenly the phone rang.

She ran down the stairs to Isaac's spotless white-tiled kitchen and answered the only phone he had, the ancient kind with a rotary dial. "Hello?"

"Who is this?" a woman's voice shouted. Zoe could hear street noises in the background; the caller was clearly on a cell.

"It's Zoe Bennett. I'm helping Isaac. May I ask who's calling, please?"

"Deb. Where is he?"

"Um, I believe it's Arizona."

"I bet," Deb said. Then the line went dead.

Zoe hung up the phone, wondering if she should have told Deb about Arizona. Well, too late now.

Then she picked up the phone again and called Dara's apartment, but there was no answer. And she didn't want to leave a message, because what would she say: *Where are you, Dara?* It made no sense to ask that if the person wasn't there to answer. And Dara didn't have a cell. Why did she need one, she once joked, when she was always with Zoe anyway?

Well, maybe she'd try calling Dara's apartment again later. From home.

"See you tomorrow, guys," she called up the stairs, smiling a little at how funny that sounded. For a second she stood at the foot of the stairs, breathing the warm, strangely soothing air of Isaac's weird apartment. Then she locked the door with her special key and hurried outside, where a blasting truck horn immediately scolded her: *Hey, Zoe! You're back in the real world now, so wake up and pay attention!*

# 6

The walls of Zoe's apartment were actually shaking.

That's how loud the music was: If you looked at the family photos in the entry (Isadora beaming as she took a curtain call, Malcolm hoisting his Math Olympiad trophy, Mom hugging Spencer a few minutes after his birth, Dad and Zoe waving from the Statue of Liberty), you could see them all twitching a little, back and forth.

Wincing, Zoe walked into the living room, where Isadora and her best friend, Nina, and some blond girl named Palmer were sprawled all over the Bennetts' ash gray sectional sofa, chanting some deafening hip-hop song to their invisible but adoring fans.

"Do you think you can turn it down a little, Isadora?" Zoe shouted. "You can practically hear it in the elevator."

"Sorry!" Isadora gracefully jumped up to switch off the CD player, but the air was still vibrating. "We were just psyching ourselves up to go audition."

"Yeah, Iz, like you really need psyching up," teased Nina. "You know you already have the lead."

"I don't!"

"Of course you do."

"Of course I *don't*," said Isadora, beaming. "Everyone's trying out, Nina. You never know."

"Ahh, but you see, my dear, I know all," said Nina. She picked up a sofa pillow and put it on her head. "I am zee swami," she said in a heavily accented voice. "I can zee into zee fu-ture."

"Nina, you are just too painfully bizarre," Palmer said. "Shut up and let Isadora pretend to worry."

"I'm not pretending," Isadora protested.

"Oh, come on, Iz. You totally have the part. Nina's telepathic."

"Clairvoyant," Zoe corrected Palmer. She looked at her sister, who was organizing her thick sandy blond hair into a sloppy ponytail. Isadora was gorgeous. She was also an amazing singer; of course she'd get the starring role. "I thought the musical was just for Middle Division."

"Upper Division too," said Isadora. "The first co-division production in Hubbard history."

*Which means it'll be harder for Dara,* Zoe thought. "But weren't tryouts right after school?"

"For Middle Div. Upper's in half an hour."

"Oh," Zoe said distractedly. "Well, I need to make a phone call now, so if you guys could please...."

"We'll keep it down, dah-ling. Never fear."

Zoe grabbed the hallway phone and locked herself in the bedroom she shared with Isadora. Then she called Dara's number again, and this time Dara picked up.

"Gasp!" Dara cried. "I'm so sorry, Zoe! I totally forgot you were waiting after school! Do you forgive me?"

Zoe sat down on her bottom bunk. "Don't be silly. Of course I do."

In the background Zoe could hear a loud voice. "Is that Zoe on the phone? Tell her you were awesome."

Dara giggled. "Leg says I was awesome."

"Leg?" Zoe repeated. "She's at your house right now?"

"Yeah, she walked me home from auditions. I'm so ecstatic, Zoe. I mean, I was just incredibly nervous. But the weird thing was, once I started singing, it was actually kind of fun!"

"Well, you have such a great voice, Dara. I've always said so, right?"

"I know, but it's totally different in front of one or two people. I mean, I never get nervous; it's like singing in front of a mirror! But this was the first time in my life I had an *actual school audience*."

Zoe smiled. "That's so cool. I'm really, really happy for you."

"Not yet! You can't be happy until I actually get a part. Say 'fingers crossed.'"

"Fingers crossed. Oh, guess what. I was just over at Isaac's, and I noticed that the baby golden gecko was peeking at me."

"Fascinating," Dara said. "But also a little bit gross, actually. How much longer are you doing that thing?"

"I'm not sure. Like a week, maybe. Oh, by the way, I thought of a good Which: Which is more repulsive, greasy hair or body odor?"

"Body odor," Dara said. "Whoops, someone's trying to call. I think it's my mom. Talk to you later."

Zoe hung up, wondering what Dara meant by "later." Was she planning to call Zoe back? Maybe after Leg went home? Or did "later" just mean, *I'm busy now, Zoe. I'll see you tomorrow at lunch?*

She lay on her bed, staring up at the swirly bedsprings of Isadora's bunk. Then suddenly she sat up. *Lucas's notebook*, she thought. She'd forgotten all about it. But Lucas probably hadn't; probably he was really worried about it by now. Probably he thought he'd never see it again.

She slipped it out of her hoodie pocket and opened the cover, this time fully prepared to see the loud warning.

> **PERSONAL PROPERTY!!! KEEP OUT!!!**
> **I'll know if you read anything.**

She opened the back cover then, but there was no other writing, not even a phone number she could call. On the last few pages Lucas had drawn something strange—not a doodle, but some sort of fantastical creature, over and over. It had a bird's beak and flowing hair and a big inhuman eye. Its stomach, or whatever it was, was decorated with a row of four perfectly round dots. Zoe counted: Lucas had drawn the creature eleven times, and every time, it was exactly the same.

She flipped to the middle pages, then back to the beginning. No other weird creatures, just more of the same incomprehensible gibberish. It was a whole notebook devoted to—well, what, exactly? She'd never know. But for some strange reason, she kept turning the pages. And when she got to page twenty, her heart froze.

⸸ɑH xⱷH ⱷbσHm̩ m̩ʙʀb ⱱⲒbⱵ bbⱷm̩ bⱷſa.

*IBD PXFA YIXK, YIXK, YIXK. FALKQ*
*IFHB EBO.*


*24 4423243325 442315 22244231*
*3311321514 ZOE 3134342543*
*2433441542154344243322.*


Her name: ZOE. Right in the middle of all that outer space language, or numbers, or whatever it was. She shut the notebook in horror. So she'd been right: He *had* been eavesdropping on her in the cafeteria! In fact, he'd probably written down every single word she'd said. It was probably all there, in some kind of crazy, demented code. Who did that little alien think he was, anyway? Did he think Zoe was some kind of lizard he could just sit in the lunchroom and "observe"?

With a shudder she imagined the rest of the page:

*"Zoe Bennett: Nibbled two thirds of tuna-and-potato-chip sandwich. Bobbed head at Dara Grosbard. Stared."*

She could hear footsteps in the hallway, so she quickly slipped the notebook under her pillow.

Then Isadora burst into the room, not even caring that Zoe had closed the door for privacy. Without a word of apology, Isadora kicked off her shoes, yanked off her top, and slipped on a skinny black V-neck with shiny gold stitching.

"Well, I'm off to tryouts," she announced. "Wish me luck, Zo."

"You really don't need any, Izzy."

"Oh, yes I do. There's so much competition for the lead this year, and I'm just incredibly nervous."

Zoe blinked. "That's exactly what Dara said: 'I was just incredibly nervous.'"

Isadora's face lit up. "You mean she finally auditioned?"

"Yeah. She did, actually." Zoe watched Isadora brush her hair. Then something occurred to her. "What do you mean, 'finally'?"

"Well, I knew she desperately wanted to, but she was always too scared."

"Really? How did you know that?"

"She told me, I think."

"*Dara* told you that? When?"

"I don't remember. Sometime last spring, maybe, when she was over here. Why? She never told you?"

Zoe shook her head.

"Well, maybe she was too embarrassed. Or too self-conscious. Or too, I don't know, *something*." Isadora slipped on a big pair of dangly earrings. "Listen, Zoe,

Dara has a fabulous voice, but what they're looking for more than anything is stage presence. And tryouts can be so cutthroat; a lot of Hubbard kids just really know how to turn it on. So try to be there for her when they post the cast list. The important thing is that she's finally brave enough to audition."

Isadora lip-glossed her mouth and made a kissy face in the mirror. She studied her reflection. "Zit city," she announced.

Then she grabbed an enormous black leather bag and slung it over her shoulder. "As for you, dah-ling, stay out of trouble, think happy thoughts, bye-bye!"

# 7

Tuesday morning Zoe was the second one up. (The first one up was Dad, who always left for his painting jobs before any other Bennett was awake.) Today Zoe was dressed for school and eating her breakfast at seven ten. Her plan was to get to school as early as possible, to find Lucas.

But just as she was finishing her waffles, her little brother Spencer marched into the kitchen. "Mom said make waffles for ME!" he yelled.

"Really? Why can't Mom do it?"

"She's ASLEEP. She said YOU had to do it, Zoe. This minute!" Spencer held out his arms like airplane wings and ran around the kitchen in little circles. "Waffles, waffles, waffles!" he sang. "With syrup, syrup, syrup!"

"Shh," Zoe said, glancing at the clock. "You'll wake up everybody else."

"Too late," grumbled Malcolm, shuffling into the kitchen. "That little monster learned how to climb up into my bunk. Which he did at precisely four thirty, Eastern Standard Time."

Zoe patted Malcolm's shoulder as he sat down in front of a bowl of Rice Krispies. Her older brother was a pain, but he was sharing a room with Spencer. That definitely earned him a few bonus points.

"Any chance you could make the little monster some waffles?" she asked hopefully.

"Why can't you?"

"Because I want to get to school early."

"You?" He shoveled cereal into his mouth. Two wet Krispies clung to his lower lip. "What for? To hang out with Dara, you mean?"

"No. Actually, Malcolm, I do other things besides hang out with Dara."

"Like what? Multiply colors? Feed frogs?"

"RIBBIT, RIBBIT, RIBBIT," shouted Spencer. "I want waffles!"

"You're *getting* them," said Zoe, burning her fingertips as she grabbed them from the toaster oven. "And Isaac doesn't even have frogs. And if you're going to tease me all the time, why should I tell you anything, Malcolm?"

"Because I am your lord and master. Bow down to me and confess all!"

"Oh, stuff it, Mal, all right?" She checked the kitchen clock again. Seven twenty-five. Now it was probably too late to see Lucas before homeroom. Well, never mind; she'd confront him about the notebook during Ancient Civs. Or better yet, at lunch. Maybe in the hallway outside the cafeteria, where she wouldn't have to shout.

Once Spencer had been fed, and she'd cleaned up the mess he'd made pouring syrup all over the table, and she'd called good-bye to her mother through the shower door, she slipped the notebook back into her hoodie pocket and walked the four blocks to school. First period was English, taught this year by Gabriel, whose eyelashes were shockingly long for a grown-up male. Practically all the girls at Hubbard had crushes on him; they called him "Babe-riel," even Isadora. Zoe was pretty sure she didn't have a crush, but her heart sort of skittered when he stopped her in the hall.

"You have that essay for me, Zoe?" he asked, smiling.

"What essay?"

"The one I assigned the second day of school. Writing a myth about yourself? Zoe-as-Olympian? You don't remember?"

"No, I do," she said quickly. "I just . . . haven't done it yet." The truth was, she couldn't figure out what to write. Briefly she'd considered turning it into a sort of joke—Zoe, goddess of color doodles, turns Malcolm, god of obnoxious comments, into cherry pi (pie?). But of course Gabriel wouldn't have understood it. Or even have thought it was funny, probably. So she'd just tried to forget the whole assignment.

"That's not okay," Gabriel said. He stopped smiling. "You know, I really don't think you're operating on all cylinders, Zoe, and I also don't think you and I are on the same page. To mix metaphors, for which I apologize. Maybe you should have a little chat with Owen."

Owen Kimball was the Head of Middle Division. He was always cheery; the kids loved him.

Zoe peeked at Gabriel's eyelashes. "You mean," she said carefully, "go have a little chat with him *now*?"

"Sure," Gabriel said. He smiled at her again. "Why not?"

Then Mackenzie came running over to tell Gabriel how she'd nearly memorized some sonnet, and he turned his back to Zoe, as if it had all been settled. Well, fine, she told herself. She'd go see Owen. Kids did it all the time.

Owen's office was on the third floor, a few doors down from Signe's classroom. She tapped lightly on the door. "I'm on the phone!" he called out. "Just two more seconds, please!"

"Okay," she called back, immediately realizing that

if he was on the phone he didn't want an answer. She looked around the tiny waiting area. The walls were layered with postcards and cartoons and incredible student artwork—abstract paintings (not doodles, though) and moody self-portraits of kids she sort of recognized. On a tadpole-shaped coffee table there were copies of the most recent editions of the *Hubbard News*, a three-times-a-year publication that bragged about all the awards and achievements of the "remarkable Hubbard community." She picked up a copy and opened it randomly: "Barrett McKay's third book of poetry was recently nominated for a National Book Award—" "Jennie Godwin's work with Siberian tigers is the subject of a new documentary—" She closed it, returned it to the pile on the tadpole table, and tucked her hair behind her ears. A minute or two later Owen called her into his office.

He was grinning, as if he were thrilled to see her. He was a small, wiry man who raced in the city marathon, his head shaven, probably to reduce wind resistance. There was something about him that was so sharp, so energetic, so opposite-of-Dad, that Zoe immediately felt uneasy.

"Well, hello, Zoe Bennett," he boomed. "Sit down and stay awhile!"

He gestured in the direction of two seating options: a

standard metal office chair pulled up alertly to his desk, or a red plastic beanbag chair squished casually against the wall. Zoe nearly dove into the friendly-looking giant beanbag, but something told her she'd be better off in the responsible-looking office chair. She sat down carefully, folding her hands in her lap.

Owen's smile flickered for a millisecond, and a strange thought flashed across her mind: *Were the chairs some kind of test? Did I just fail?*

"So, Zoe," he said, leaning way back in his own leather desk chair. "I was actually hoping you'd stop by. I'm hearing from Gabriel that you owe him some work. And Anya tells me you've been drawing pictures in Math. And Signe says she isn't seeing anything from you. Which surprises me, because kids here typically find her inspiring."

"I'm sorry." She'd been slumping. Now she forced herself to sit perfectly straight, which meant the back of the metal chair was digging into her spine. *I definitely should have chosen the beanbag!* she thought.

Owen studied her for a long, agonizing moment. "Here's my dilemma, Zoe," he said finally as he leaned across his desk. "I just this minute had a phone call from a dad whose daughter is a world-class violinist. This girl wants to go to Hubbard, and I had to tell the dad that we're at capacity. Which is terrific. It's our goal, in fact. But I have to ask myself: Are we filling our Middle Division with the most deserving students? The kind who'll make the most of everything Hubbard has to offer? Would you like a glass of water?"

"What? No, thank you."

"Okay," he said. "Let me make this plain, Zoe. You're not in Lower Division anymore. Expectations have changed. It's time to fully engage yourself in Hubbard, or else consider other options." He pointed to a gaudy papier-mâché puppet slouching awkwardly on his bookshelf, and smiled in a way that was probably meant to be jokey. "Hey, you don't want to go through life like that guy over there. With us, but not really animate."

He was calling her a *puppet*? "Okay," she said stupidly. "I understand."

He knit his eyebrows. "You all right, then, Zoe?"

"Terrific," she said.

Then she got up out of the horrible chair and ran out of Owen's office, down the hall to the third-floor bathroom, where she burst into hot, humiliated tears. The day had started so normally: Waffles—frogs—eyelashes. And now Owen was—what? Calling her names? Threatening to kick her out? Where would she even go? Some normal place that had bells and red pens? The only school she'd ever known—the only school any of the Bennetts had ever known—was Hubbard. Even Spencer went to Hubbard Preschool! What would Mom and Dad say when they heard: *Oh, Zoe, why didn't you? Oh, Zoe, how could you? Oh, Zoe, didn't you realize what a special, special place this was?*

She turned on the tap and flooded her face with cold water. She had to see Dara. Dara would understand everything. Just talking to her would help Zoe think straight.

But first, somehow, she'd have to get through the rest of the morning.

# 8

At lunch Zoe didn't even bother getting her tuna-and-potato-chip sandwich. She just headed straight for Dara's table and sat there for a few seconds, unable to talk.

"Gasp," Dara said, her big gray-blue eyes looking worried. "Are you okay, Zoe?"

"No. This is the worst day in my life."

"What happened?"

Before Zoe could answer, Leg and Paloma came over with trays heaped with salad and sat down right next to Dara.

"Sorry," Zoe said immediately. "This is private."

"Hey, don't let us stop you," Paloma said, trading glances with Leg.

Dara rubbed Zoe's arm. "Oh, come on, Zoe. If it's really important, you don't want to talk about it here, right? I mean, not if it's private. We'll talk about it later, okay?"

Zoe stared at her. This was The Worst Day in Zoe's Life and Dara wanted to talk about it *later*? How could she be so insensitive?

And then instantly Zoe realized Dara was right. Because even if those awful girls weren't sitting there, this was the stupidest possible place to be talking about Owen. Zoe would have to shout the entire story: *HE THREATENED TO KICK ME OUT. AND THEN HE CALLED ME A PUPPET*. Everyone in Middle Division would hear. What a fiasco that would be.

Dara was actually protecting her. She was a true friend, and Zoe, as usual, was a total idiot.

"Okay, sure," she heard herself saying. "Later."

Dara smiled, and Zoe could feel her own face staring to relax.

"So, Dara," Leg said teasingly. "Have they posted the cast list yet?"

"Not yet," Dara said. "Soon, I think."

"Are you psyched?"

"A little. I'm trying not to get my hopes up."

"Are you nervous? Don't be nervous."

"I'm going to get some lunch," Zoe announced. She stood up and glanced at Dara's empty tray. "You want anything?"

"No, thanks. I'm actually not that hungry."

"Because you're nervous," Paloma said, sticking out her tongue. "Or do you just want to look sexy in your costume?"

Zoe could feel her teeth clench at that. But now that Paloma mentioned it, she could see that Dara did look a little pale. "You should try to eat something," she urged Dara. "I'll see what's in the kitchen."

Leg smiled. "As long as you're up, Zoe, I'd like an apple. If it isn't bruised."

"I'll look," Zoe said, thinking: *No, I won't.*

She walked into the kitchen and helped herself to the usual: sandwich wrapped in cellophane, bag of chips, pint of chocolate milk. She also took a big chocolate chip cookie to split with Dara. She was just about to get herself a straw when she noticed Lucas. He was sitting at the weirdo table, but obviously not to hang out with Ezra, who was listening to his iPod and reading one of his warfare books. Lucas was definitely on his own, all hunched over like a little—No. She'd been about to think *gargoyle*, but she stopped herself. That was Tyler's word, and it was horrible.

Suddenly she remembered that she still had Lucas' crazy notebook. It didn't seem very important anymore, not after everything that had happened this morning, but she needed to give it back. And she probably still needed to talk to him. And anyway, it wasn't as if she were in a huge hurry to get back to Leg and Paloma.

"Hi, Lucas," she said, sitting down next to him. "I have something for you. Here." She reached into her hoodie pocket and pulled out the spiral notebook.

He snatched it from her. "How did you get it?"

"You left it behind. When you ran out of the lobby yesterday. After school. Remember?"

"Yeah. Um, thanks."

"You're welcome. But listen. I noticed you were writing about me, and I really want you to stop."

He looked startled. "What makes you think I was writing about *you*?"

"Because I read my name. I'm sorry," she added. "I know your notebook is private property."

He shook his head impatiently. "Where did you see your name? In my notebook. Exactly, I mean."

"I don't know. There were all these weird drawings in the back and then in the front there were these, I don't know, languages, but on one page you wrote 'Zoe'. *Z-O-E*. I'm positive I saw it."

He was staring right at her now. "You read *ciphers*?"

"What?"

"You just said you read your name. Which was in cipher. See?"

He flipped through the notebook, then thrust it at her.

She stared at the open page: the same outer space gibberish as yesterday. Only this time, no "Zoe." How was that possible? Had he written it in disappearing ink?

She shoved the notebook back at him. "I don't understand. When I saw it yesterday—"

"You deciphered your name! *Z-O-E.* Did you realize you can *do* that?"

"Of course I can't," Zoe said, alarmed at his excitement. "Don't be ridiculous."

"You're a natural cryptanalyst! Some people are just *like* that. It's actually a form of genius. Or brain damage, arguably."

"Okay, Lucas, now you're totally hallucinating. And you'd better stop writing about me, all right?"

"So is this your new boyfriend, Zoe?" someone asked loudly. It was Leg; she was holding an apple. Paloma was right beside her, grinning. Dara was standing in back of them both, biting her thumbnail.

"Shut up, Leg," Zoe snapped, feeling her cheeks start to burn.

For a moment no one said anything.

Suddenly Lucas laughed. "'Shut up, Leg.' What a bizarre English sentence. Just think how that would translate into any other human language. 'Shut-up-leg.'"

Then he stood and left the table without even emptying his tray.

Zoe started to giggle; she couldn't help it. Dara frowned at her meaningfully, but she pretended not to see.

Leg shrugged. "Well, he's certainly a sick little puppy," she declared. Then she took a bite of her apple, examined it critically, and tossed it into the trash.

## 9

The last class of the day was Ancient Civilizations. When Zoe arrived at the classroom, she saw that Lucas was already seated at his desk, ignoring her as he wrote in his spiral notebook. She took her own seat quickly. Immediately she noticed that on her whiteboard desk someone had responded to her tiny message from yesterday.

> *4 = Blue.*
> **What is 5?**

Without thinking she reached for her dry erase marker and wrote:

> *Green.*

Then she looked up at Lucas. But he just kept ignoring her, or pretending to ignore her. *Well, fine,* Zoe thought. Why should she want to discuss her theory with him anyway? She pushed her curls out of her face and waited quietly for her classmates to take their seats.

And then she tried her hardest to pay attention to Signe's lesson. And not just pay attention—*look* like she was paying attention. She didn't doodle once. She just kept her eyes riveted on her teacher (who today was wearing an enormous shawl the color of pistachio ice cream), trying to nod and smile every once in awhile, as if she felt inspired by everything Signe was saying.

But it was hopeless. Signe never looked at Zoe; she only seemed to notice Lucas. She was showing slides about ancient Egypt, and he kept interrupting to inform her that it was *not* Ptolemy the astronomer who was a member of the royal family, and that hieroglyphics were typically written right to left and top to bottom but were occasionally also written left to right, or bottom to top. Once Ezra Blecker tried to get into the discussion, making some impressive-sounding comment about the Egyptians' early use of armored siege weaponry, but Lucas cut him off midsentence. "Actually," he called out, "that's historically inaccurate."

Ezra looked startled. "No, it isn't," he protested. "I read it in a book. It was called *War and Warfare in Ancient Egypt,* and it was by—"

"Some hack," Lucas finished, smiling cheerfully. "Who couldn't even read hieroglyphics, frankly."

Usually people didn't stick up for Ezra, but this was really too much.

"Oh, yeah, Lucas?" Jake called out. "And how do you know he couldn't read hieroglyphics?"

Lucas shrugged. "Because I can."

Jake knew six languages, but he didn't know hieroglyphics, so he didn't challenge Lucas further. As for Ezra, Zoe noticed that he appeared to be taking notes, but maybe he was just writing "Shut up, Lucas" all over his whiteboard desk. The strange thing was, Signe just kept beaming and saying "Thank you, Lucas, thank you," as if she were absolutely delighted with this obnoxious kid, who didn't even notice that the other kids were groaning, and that Leg sniggered every time he opened his mouth.

At dismissal, Zoe headed for the lockers, hoping to find Dara there so she could finally tell her about the "little chat" with Owen. But then she heard Mackenzie excitedly announce that the cast list was about to be posted "any minute." Which meant that Dara wouldn't want to go somewhere private—and also, understandably, that Dara would be too distracted to listen. And Zoe couldn't bear to hang around Hubbard waiting for her friend again. Not after yesterday. And not after today.

So she slipped out of the building without saying

good-bye to anyone. The air outside was damp and refreshing; it felt almost like swimming pool water, the way it feels when you first jump in.

And unexpectedly, Zoe found herself thinking about third grade.

Late in the spring of Zoe's third-grade year, Hubbard had announced that it was opening its Olympic-size swimming pool in the afternoons "for Lower Division enjoyment." *Enjoyment. How nice of them*, Zoe had thought happily. But of course everything in the Lower Division was about "fun" and "joy" and "discovery" and "exploration," so it wasn't terribly shocking to receive the unrequested gift of an enormous pool. Now, of course, she realized that Donovan, the Head of Recreation Arts, had actually been using the Lower Division swim sessions to evaluate students for the highly competitive Middle Division swim program. But in third grade Zoe had simply taken them at their word and stayed after school three days a week to "enjoy" the turquoise water.

She couldn't swim. She didn't care. All she wanted to do was splash around in the shallow end with Dara. They'd invented a fascinating game about two sisters named Aurora (Zoe) and Arabella (Dara) who'd escaped from their evil uncle and were hiding out on a tropical island. For some unknowable reason Jake and Mackenzie began hanging around in the shallow end too, every once in a while splashing them or diving underwater to grab their feet. Zoe was annoyed, but Dara started splashing them back and laughing, and pretty soon they had key roles in the story: Mackenzie as the underwater goddess Hydranna (which sounded to Zoe ridiculously like *hydrant*, but she didn't say anything), and Jake as the cunning and powerful supervillain Tidal Wave.

For the rest of third grade, and then for about the first half of fourth, the four kids continued the game, "enjoying" Hubbard's wonderful pool exactly as they'd been invited. Even Zoe had to admit to herself that the game was just as fun with more characters (although Jake kept showing off his underwater technique, and occasionally, as Tidal Wave, splashed them in their eyes).

But then one day Donovan blew his whistle and called Jake and Mackenzie over for a friendly conversation. He'd been watching them play, he told them, and he thought they had "real potential" as "serious swimmers." Would they be interested in a few casual, no-big-deal swimming lessons? Yes, of course they would. This meant abandoning Zoe and Dara to play the game by themselves, but that was just fine with Zoe anyway.

So they played it for a couple of weeks, just the two of them: Aurora and Arabella, who by now had each assumed a few of the abandoned superpowers. And then one afternoon, just as they were preparing a tidal wave defense against the recently-returned-from-the-dead evil uncle, Donovan blew his whistle. "Dara," he called, "can I see you for a minute?"

"Be right back," called Dara as she swam over to Donovan's lifeguard chair and pulled herself out of the water.

From the shallow end Zoe could lip-read the conversation. Donovan was telling Dara that she, too, had "real potential" as a "serious swimmer," and was offering her the chance for some casual, no-big-deal swimming lessons. Dara had her back turned, so her response was harder to read, but she appeared to be nodding as if she were saying yes. *And really*, thought Zoe, *why wouldn't she?* Everybody else seemed to jump at the chance to swim with Donovan, who not so very long ago had actually qualified for the U.S. Olympic team.

Zoe closed her eyes. She floated on her back a little, one of the few pool maneuvers she could sort of do.

*Sooner or later, everyone goes off and seriously swims,* she told herself. *Except for me. I'm the only one left in the shallow end. And I don't even care one subatomic bit!*

There was a splash. Zoe opened her eyes. Dara was back, grinning.

"Where were we?" she was asking. "In the game, I mean."

"I don't remember," Zoe lied. "Anyway, so what did Donovan say?"

"Nothing important. Just if I wanted some boring swimming lessons." She dove underwater and gracefully circled Zoe's legs. Zoe watched her, astonished. Somehow, until that very moment, she had never realized how well Dara could swim.

Finally Dara resurfaced. "Well?" Zoe asked quickly, before Dara could pop underwater again. "What did you tell him? Do you?"

"Oh, yawn," said Dara, who was just starting to talk that smiley-face way. "Of course I don't, Zoe. Why would I? Let's just play the game."

Now Zoe shivered slightly inside her hoodie.

*Could it be,* she asked herself, *that Dara has gone off to seriously swim? Leaving me behind in the shallow water?*

*She wouldn't just do that.*

*I'm sure she wouldn't.*

Finally Zoe arrived at Isaac's brownstone. And when she let herself into his house with her special key, she sighed deeply, the first calm breaths she'd taken all day.

First she fed everybody. Isaac had supplied her with a few days' worth of crickets, leaving her some money for the pet store when she ran out. He'd also left three big plastic bags in the refrigerator, one with escarole and collard greens; the second with apple, banana, and mango slices; and the third with chunks of butternut squash and carrots. He hadn't given her a phone number for his mother's house in Arizona, but he had given her an e-mail address if she needed to contact him. She was supposed to use Dad's computer and his e-mail account, Dad had said. But Isaac wanted to hear from her only in an emergency. "I don't want to be bothered with trivialities," he'd warned her.

Well, sure. She wasn't here to waste her time on "trivialities," anyway. Her job was to mist and water the non-desert-dwellers, distribute fresh leaves and food, maybe take a few notes. And watch: spot the baby golden gecko hiding in the leaves, connect the dots on the backs of the salamanders. At one point she thought she might have heard somebody chirp, but no, she'd probably just imagined it. Because lizards didn't have their own private language, did they? *Just observe*, she urged herself, imagining Isaac's disapproval.

But of course it was almost impossible to shut off her imagination completely, and as she walked from tank to tank, she found herself wondering: Did lizards have feelings? Did the brown basilisk ever feel jealous because the black-spotted newt was hanging out with the iguanas? Did the green anole ever threaten to kick the brown anole out of the tank? Or did they just stare at each other all day and bob their heads and eat bugs?

Maybe it would be better to be a lizard. Or to be like Isaac, whose whole life was just wire and reptiles.

She stayed with the lizards for almost an hour. Finally she came downstairs, just as a child's voice was talking on Isaac's message machine: "Hi, Daddy? It's Willie. I miss you. Here's Mommy." And then, "Where's that check, Isaac? If I don't get it by tomorrow, I'm calling my lawyer!"

It sounded like Deb. Well, it was a good thing Zoe hadn't heard the phone ringing this time, because Deb sure didn't sound happy. She wondered what Isaac had done to make Deb so mad at him. Maybe she didn't like reptiles.

Zoe locked Isaac's front door with her key. For a

moment she stood on the landing, taking another deep breath of the damp, refreshing September air. And then she nearly jumped.

Because there was Lucas, sitting on the bottom front step of the brownstone.

He was wearing that awful brown tweed coat again. And again he was hunched over gargoyle-style, reading something that looked like a field guide. As soon as he saw her, he sprang up.

"Oh, hi, Zoe," he said eagerly. "So I was thinking: You want me to teach you some cipher languages? Or coding? Which is a completely different thing, actually."

"What? No, thanks. And what are you doing here, Lucas? Are you *following* me?"

"Well, I just wanted to talk to you, so I waited for you to come out."

"You mean you've been sitting here a whole *hour*?"

"That's okay. I was reading." He looked at his sneakers, which were some unrecognizable brand and extremely filthy. "You live here?"

"No."

"Visiting?"

"Sort of. Pet-sitting."

"For what?"

"This guy. A kind of friend of my dad's."

"No," said Lucas, grinning. "I mean, what kind of animal?"

Zoe sighed. "None of your business, okay? Lizards."

"I hate lizards," Lucas said cheerfully. "There were tons of them in Guatemala, and they crawled all over the place. While you were sleeping, even. Disgusting. But I always kind of liked geckoes, even though it's weird how they never blink. You know anything about ancient military codes?"

"What? Of course I don't." For the first time, Zoe studied Lucas's face. With his upturned nose, freckled cheeks, and long, sun-bleached hair, he looked almost a full year younger than everyone else in the sixth grade. She didn't want to be mean to him, she really didn't. But still.

"Listen, Lucas," she said evenly, as she started down the steps. "I know you're just trying to be friendly, but why don't you talk to Ezra or Jake Greiner or somebody like that?"

"Because you deciphered your *name*, Zoe! That's incredibly unusual! Don't you even *care*?"

She stopped on the sidewalk. "It was just a coincidence. Maybe I wanted to read my name. Or maybe I imagined it. I don't know. But I'm sure it doesn't mean anything, and

I think you're kind of overreacting." She glanced down the street and added, "And anyway, I'm not some baby secret agent with a decoder ring."

"Yeah, well, neither am I!" He tilted his pointy chin at her.

"Okay, sorry," she said quickly. "Look, I'm not trying to hurt your feelings. I'm just really, really busy right now." When he didn't respond, she added, "Actually, I'm going to meet my best friend, Dara."

"No, you're not."

"Excuse me?"

"You're not going to meet Dara. She's off with that horrible Leg person, and that other girl, the super-nasty one."

"You mean Paloma?"

"Right, Paloma. I saw them all leave school together. They were laughing really hard. And I don't think Dara is your best friend, frankly."

"Oh, yeah? Well, who cares *what* you think." Her dark eyes flashed. "You know what, Lucas? Maybe you know a ton about hieroglyphics, but you don't know anything about Dara. Or anything about me, either."

"Actually, Zoe, that's wrong. Well, half-wrong; I think I know *you* fairly well." Suddenly Lucas reached into his pocket and pulled out his red mechanical pencil and his little spiral notebook. Then he wrote something, tore out the page, and handed it to her.

"What's this?" she asked, frowning.

"You tell me."

She squinted at the tiny paper.

> *EEEHEIEE EEZEEEOEEE EIE*
> *EEBEEETE EYEEOEEU ECEEEAEENEE*
> *EEREEAEEDEEE EEEETEEHEIEESEEE*

"It says 'Hi Zoe I bet you can read this,'" Zoe muttered. "You just take out the extra *E*'s."

"The extra letters are called nulls," he said, writing something else. "Try this."

> *OSA YCANY OUSE EBYT HEDA WNSEA*
> *RLYLI GHTW HATSOP—*

"'The Star Spangled Banner.' With spaces messed up."

"Very good. And this?"

> *SBSSMASL ELSTTSSIL SA SSDASH*
> *YSRASMS*

"Mary had a little lamb. Backward with *S*'s. Why are you bothering me with this stupid garbage?"

"Why?" He was beaming at her now. "Because this proves it, Zoe. I knew it: You're just like me."

"I'm not," she snapped. "You're demented. And you know what else, Lucas? Don't follow me, don't write about me in your crazy languages, and don't even talk to me. Just totally stay away from now on, okay?"

Then she turned and fled.

# 10

About a block from her apartment Zoe slowed way down.

Because who really cared about that weirdo Lucas, or his stupid hallucinations. Or what he thought about Dara, either. She had more important things to worry about.

What if, by the time she got home, Owen had called her parents? What if they were so upset they left work early to come home and have phase two of the "little chat"? Maybe they'd be sitting on the living room sofa when she walked in the door: Mom in her white orthodontist jacket, Dad in his paint-spattered jeans. Maybe, as she tried to slip down the hallway to her bedroom, they'd call out something casual like, *Zoe? May we please see you for a minute?*

She had to face them sometime, of course. But after that psychotic conversation with Lucas just now, all she really wanted to do was call Dara. And if that was impossible—if Dara really was with horrible Leg—then she didn't feel like talking to anybody. Especially her parents, who were definitely not going to be thrilled with what Owen had to say.

She opened her apartment door, hoping to hear hip-hop music, signifying no adults. But the apartment was strangely quiet. She walked into the living room. There was Isadora, sitting on the sofa with a funny, almost frozen, look on her face. Zoe's heart leapt.

She tried to steel herself. "Are Mom and Dad here?"

"No, but they're on their way," Isadora said. Then she burst into tears.

Immediately Zoe ran to the sofa and threw her arms around her sister. Was Isadora getting kicked out of Hubbard too? *Don't be stupid,* Zoe scolded herself. Then what could it possibly mean? She'd never seen Isadora like this before. Ever.

Finally she said, "You want me to get you a tissue, Izzy?"

Isadora nodded. Her face looked pink and puffy, like a partially inflated balloon.

Zoe got up and returned with a nearly empty box of Kleenex and a roll of paper towels. "What happened?" she asked softly.

"It's just too awful to talk about."

"What is? Tell me."

Isadora grabbed a tissue from the box. "It doesn't matter!" she wailed. "I don't even care!"

Then she honked her nose and threw the wadded-up tissue onto the sofa. "Palmer stole my part," she finally blurted out. "The one I absolutely *had*."

"Who's Palmer?"

"You don't remember? She was sitting right here in this living room just yesterday. Skinny, dyed blond hair, two faces..."

"Oh, right." Who'd said "telepathic." When she'd really meant "clairvoyant."

"Of course, darling Palmer *claimed* she wasn't even planning to try out. But then somehow she managed to read for the lead. And this afternoon, when the cast list was up, there she was, in big letters, right at the very top. Oh, and by the way, Zoe, *your* friend got a really great part."

"You mean Dara?"

"Of course Dara. Who else?" asked Isadora irritably. "Wake up, Zoe." She leaned back into the sofa and closed her eyes. Her nose was starting to run, Zoe saw.

"You want some paper towel?" Zoe asked, offering the roll. "It's not great, but I think we're out of tissue."

Isadora wiped her nose with her hand. "I know you're not an actor, Zoe, so let me tell you something major: No part in a play is ever worth betraying a friend. I don't care if it's a lead, *you just don't do it*. Hubbard is full of übertalented people who get this, but not, apparently, darling Palmer."

She wiped her hand off on her track pants. Then she wiped her nose with her other hand. "You're so lucky to be friends with someone like Dara. She'd never act like this."

Zoe nodded. "You want some water? Or some Diet Coke, maybe? I think there's an open bottle in the fridge."

"No. Stop fetching things, Zoe! Just sit with me, okay?" Then Isadora started crying again, and Zoe began to despair. She wished there were something she could think of to say, something wise and comforting. But she was hopeless with words; she'd always been. And now it seemed Isadora didn't feel like talking, anyway.

So Zoe just sat with her on the sofa. A few minutes later Dad was home. He'd brought Isadora a bunch of yellow roses, which actually made her smile a little. But then Mom walked in the door, and Isadora burst into tears all over again.

"I *hate* that Palmer," she wailed. "She stole my part!"

"Maybe she didn't steal it from you, baby," Mom said soothingly. She hadn't even taken off her orthodontist jacket yet, as she stood in the living room stroking

Isadora's matted hair. "Maybe she just wanted her own chance to shine."

"She didn't! She's just a snake! I hate her!"

"Palmer's really horrible, Mom," Zoe explained. "She sat here yesterday on the sofa and didn't even tell Izzy she was trying out."

Mom smiled at Zoe. "Thanks, sweetheart. I'm sure Izzy will tell me all about it herself, when she's ready. But right now I think she needs some private time, okay?" She put her arm around Isadora's shoulders and led her into the grown-up bedroom, closing the door behind them as if Zoe were some kind of babyish distraction.

Then Malcolm showed up from his Math Olympiad practice, and Zoe had to answer a thousand penetrating questions about Isadora. ("What did Izzy mean, it was her part? Did the director say it was her part?") And then ten minutes later Spencer raced into the living room shouting "NO, I WON'T," followed frantically by his after-preschool babysitter Bella, who'd graduated from Hubbard five years ago and was now, except for what she stole from the Bennetts' refrigerator, a starving artist.

"DON'T HUG SPENCER," Bella was calling ahead of her. "HE'S ALL STICKY."

"I'M NOT ALL STICKY," Spencer shouted. He raced

over and gave Dad a big hug. "Bella's all sticky. Not me."

Dad looked down at his shirt. "Ahem," he said.

"I'm really sorry," Bella apologized breathlessly, plopping into a chair. "The other kid—Cameron—was holding this enormous container of Elmer's glue, and then Spencer—I mean out of nowhere—just grabbed it out of his hands, and then it went flying all over the place, not just on Spencer, but I mean all over their rug—"

"Yikes," said Dad. "How bad was the damage?"

"Pret-ty bad," said Bella, patting her chest a couple of times to catch her breath. "It was an antique. Turkish, I think."

"Was?" demanded Malcolm.

"Is," Bella corrected herself. "It's not destroyed, or anything. Just all gummy."

"Oh, boy," said Dad. "Well, I guess I'd better call them and offer to pay for something. Do you have their phone number, Bella?"

"Not on me. But they're probably in the Hubbard directory."

Dad went off to fetch the directory. Zoe turned to her little brother, who all this time had been calmly reassembling his wooden train set. "Spencer, why do you do things like that?"

"Oh, come on, Zo. It was an accident," said Malcolm. "He didn't mean it."

"Cameron has a puppy," Spencer explained. He zoomed his engine through a covered bridge, making *pfft-pfft* noises to show it was letting off steam.

"So what?" Zoe said. "You think that means you get to spill glue all over—"

"And I want one," Spencer continued. He attached a few coal cars. "A orange one. Named Six."

Malcolm laughed. "Six? That's a really dumb name, Spence."

"It's not a dumb name! *You're* a dumb name!" Suddenly the train violently derailed. Spencer dove under the table to rescue the scattered coal cars, leaving a few flakes of Elmer's glue on the polished wood floor.

Everyone turned helplessly to Dad, who had finally located the Hubbard directory in the kitchen utility drawer. "Okay, Spence, so why are you naming something Six?" he asked distractedly.

"Because orange is six. Zoe said so."

"I don't get it," Bella said. "Why did Zoe say—"

"Long story," Malcolm said. He grinned mischievously at his sister. "Spencer's right. That *is* what you said, Zo. Remember? One is white, two is whatever, three is—"

"Shut up, Malcolm," Zoe warned.

"Five is puke green—"

"I said shut up. It was *emerald* green, for your information, and anyway, it was just a theory, and I must have been crazy to even tell you."

"Oh, come on, Zozo," Dad said, glancing up from the directory. "You know we loved your theory—"

"Theory?" Bella repeated. "What about, Zoe?"

"Numbers. How they're really just colors," Malcolm said, laughing.

"Oh, awesome," said Bella. "You know, there's a word for that, Zoe!"

"There sure is," Malcolm agreed.

Zoe flashed her eyes at him, then turned to her younger brother. "And you're not getting a dog, Spencer, but even if you were, you're not naming him Six or Sixteen or any other number for that matter, because it's not even your theory in the first place."

Spencer burst into angry tears. "IT'S MY DOG!" he shouted. He picked up two coal cars and flung them across the dining room.

"Oh, well," said Bella. "I guess I'll be off now. That is, if you're absolutely sure you don't need me."

Dad smiled tiredly. "We're fine, Bella. See you tomorrow."

Then Zoe stormed into her bedroom and plopped onto her bottom bunk. Why was she even in this family? They didn't appreciate the first thing about her. Or understand her. Nobody did. Not her parents. Not her teachers. Not Owen (who apparently hadn't called). Definitely not Lucas! Dara understood, of course, but where was she? Still with Leg? She hadn't even called, and now The Worst Day in Zoe's Life was getting worse and worse by the second. If that was humanly possible.

Zoe closed her eyes.

*Think about something else,* she urged herself. *Something random.*

*Lizards. Arizona.*

*Why is that even a word? Arizona. Anozira. Zoriana.*

*Zoriana is a very cool name. But maybe for a superhero, not for an actual place.*

She thought about Isaac suddenly. Wherever he was—Arizona or Zoriana or Mars, for all she knew—he needed to hear about Deb. Even though he'd said that thing about not wanting to hear "trivialities." But Deb's phone calls didn't sound trivial to Zoe. In fact, he probably should hear about them right way.

She sighed. The last thing she felt like doing right

now was getting out of bed and explaining all this to anyone in her family. But she really had no choice, did she? This wasn't about her. Or about any other Bennett, although they'd have a hard time comprehending that.

She walked into the kitchen, where Dad was stirring something weird-smelling at the stove.

"Okay if I send Isaac an e-mail?" she asked, scrunching up her nose.

"Not now, Zozo. I'm doing Spicy Ghana Stew. New improved recipe." He started chopping up some bulb-shaped yellowish vegetable and tossing it into the big pot.

"But it's really, really important, Dad."

"Fine," he said over his shoulder. "Just leave it in my Outbox, okay?"

She nodded. Then she opened the door to the tiny office/studio where Dad worked when he was home. She clicked on his e-mail account and typed:

> Dear Mr. Wakefield,
>     Sorry to bother you, but Deb called
> 2 times. She said if she doesn't get a check
> from you she'll call her lawyer. She sounded
> upset, and that's an observation, not an
> overheated preteen reaction.

*Very truly yours,*
*Zoe Bennett*

She read it over. Then she deleted everything in the last sentence after the word "upset," hit Send, and quietly went back to her bedroom and shut the door.

# 11

On Wednesday morning at school Tyler Russo was standing a little too close to Lucas's locker.

"How's it going, Gargoyle?" he asked loudly. "No post-traumatic stress?"

Lucas blushed, but he looked Tyler right in the eye, and lifted his pointy chin defiantly. "Gargoyles, at least real ones on medieval cathedrals, are incapable of stress disorders," he replied. "They were fashioned out of stone. So really the question you're asking is nonsensical."

"Whatever," Tyler said. He grinned at the kids who'd begun to gather around Lucas's locker.

"Moreover," Lucas continued, "technically all gargoyles are waterspouts. So if you're referring to someone as 'a non-water-spouting stone carving,' which is I believe your intention, you should call that person a 'grotesque.'"

"Or a freak," Tyler suggested helpfully.

Everybody laughed.

"Oh, do tell us more, Dr. Info," Leg said in a high voice. "We're ever so enthralled."

Now Zoe could tell that her own cheeks were burning. But she didn't feel obligated to rescue Lucas. Not after the crazy way he'd followed her yesterday, and all that stuff he'd said about Dara.

And that wasn't even counting his delusion about *her*. Which was maybe the weirdest thing about this weirdo kid.

Still, she watched out of the corner of her eye as he shut his locker hurriedly and then half-ran away, head down. Why did he have to act like such a jerk in front of the other kids? Did he think they *wouldn't* pick on him if he kept showing off like that? Even at Hubbard, where everyone was an expert in something, Lucas was crossing some very obvious line.

Suddenly she heard Leg squeal. "Omigod! What *is* this?"

Her locker was open, and she was waving around a small strip of white paper. Everyone crowded to get a look, including Zoe.

Someone had written in perfectly formed letters:

*Cause division among them.*

—*Sun Tzu,*
The Art of War

"What's *that* about?" Leg demanded. "Cause division among who?"

"Nobody," Paloma said. "It's just some stupid fortune cookie."

Mackenzie shook her head. "Fortune cookies are always typed. Or printed. This is handwritten."

"Are you sure?" Tyler said. "It kind of looks like a computer font. You know, a handwriting one."

"But it's not." Mackenzie smudged the ink with her index finger. "See?"

"It's still stupid," Paloma said scornfully. "Just forget about it, Leg."

Jake grabbed the paper out of Leg's hand. He held it up to the light, as if he were checking for fingerprints. "Well, it means *something*," he insisted. "Because why would someone choose this quotation? 'Cause division'—you think that's about *math*? And why write it so carefully? And then put it in Leg's locker? Why her?"

Paloma grinned. "Maybe whoever wrote it has a crush on Leg."

"Please," Leg said, smiling.

"Maybe it's Ezra."

Jake snorted. "Ezra? You think Ezra Blecker has a crush on *Leg*?"

"Who knows," Paloma said. "Nothing would surprise me about that mute little creep. And *The Art of War*—isn't that the kind of warfare-strategy-thing he reads all the time?"

"Okay," Mackenzie said skeptically. "But why would Ezra stick a note about causing division in Leg's locker? I mean, even if he does have a crush."

"Oh, stop it, you guys," Leg said. She shut her locker. "I adore Ezra, I really do, but we're just good friends, I swear."

Everybody laughed at that.

Then Leg and Paloma walked off together, giggling. "Oh, I *know*," Zoe could hear Leg say.

Zoe frowned. She walked over to Dara, who was carefully taking her Chinese textbook out of her locker. "Were you listening to that just now?"

Dara nodded. "Uh-huh. That was incredibly weird."

"It was just some dumb note. Why did Leg have to make such a big deal about it?"

"Well," Dara said slowly. "It's her locker, right? So I guess it's a big deal to her."

"I know. But I mean, it really isn't fair to blame Ezra without any proof. Or to make fun of him like that."

Dara widened her big blue-gray eyes. "So you're

sticking up for Ezra Blecker? Why would you even do that? Besides, how much proof do we need?"

"We?"

"Groan," Dara said. "Don't be like that, Zoe."

"Don't be like what?" She stared at Dara. "You mean, just because Leg and Paloma say, 'Okay, everybody, blame weirdo Ezra,' I should?"

"I mean," Dara said quietly, "that you should stop being so jealous about Leg. Truthfully? It's getting slightly out of control."

Zoe could feel her throat start to tighten. "I'm not jealous, Dara. I'm really not! I just wish . . ." But what could she say? *I just wish we were in all the same classes again. I just wish you saved us a private lunch table. I just wish you weren't so busy after school. I just wish you'd called yesterday to ask about The Worst Day in My Life.* "I guess I just wish Leg wasn't around all the time."

"Well, I can't help it if she likes me, Zoe. Or that she's dancing in the musical, which, frankly, you don't even seem to care about."

"What? How can you say that? Of course I care about it, Dara!"

"Then how come you haven't even asked about my part?" Dara shut her locker door. It made a firm little click sound. "You know what? I can't deal with this right now," she said. Then she turned away.

For the rest of the morning Zoe doodled like crazy. She didn't care how it looked to her teachers; she just needed something to take her mind off Dara. (And of course, her own stupidity. Because how *could* she have forgotten to ask Dara about the play?) Anya walked by Zoe's desk once and put her hand on Zoe's shoulder, but she didn't whisper anything or take the paper away, so Zoe just kept drawing tornadoes in Prismacolor red. She even tried to doodle some emerald green reptiles, but the best she could do was a skink shaped like the number five. Then she decided that it didn't look anything like the skinks in Isaac's collection, so she crumpled up the page and stuck it into her backpack.

At lunch she sat at the weirdo table next to Ezra. (Dara was huddled with Leg and Paloma and some other kids who were probably in the musical, so Zoe didn't even consider sitting there.) Today Ezra was wearing a T-shirt that said DON'T MAKE ME GET MY NINJAS, and he was reading some thick book with "invasion" in the title. And he was listening to his iPod, so Zoe didn't want to interrupt him to ask how his book was.

She absently poked her potato chips into her tuna fish sandwich.

All of a sudden, Ezra pulled out his earpiece and turned to her.

"I don't like Leg," he announced.

"Excuse me?"

"Everybody keeps asking. So in case you were about to ask, I'm saving you the trouble."

"I wasn't going to, Ezra. I never, ever thought—"

"Good," he muttered, and stuck his earpiece back in.

Well, that was probably all the conversation Zoe was going to get out of him, she realized. But at least he knew she wasn't going to tease him. Or accuse him of writing fortune-cookie notes. She nibbled a bite of crunchy sandwich. Then she tried to peek at Dara. What if, she asked herself, I just went over there and apologized? *I'm sorry I forgot to ask about the play, Dara, but after all, you forgot to ask about Owen.* That wouldn't work, and anyway it would just make everybody at Dara's table look up at her and ask: *Oh, Zoe, did something happen with Owen?* And then she'd have to shout *YES, ACTU-ALLY. HE CALLED ME A PUPPET.*

She sipped some chocolate milk, which today, for some reason, seemed babyishly sweet. *Why do I keep drinking this?* she asked herself, pushing it away. All of a sudden she felt a poke from behind. And then something dropped onto her tray.

It was a folded-up piece of paper.

She spun around. Lucas was standing behind her with his arms crossed.

"What's this?" she asked, not touching it.

He grinned. "Try to figure it out, Zoe."

She unfolded the paper and frowned. It was just a bunch of shapes, different from the notebook writing, but just as strange.

⊓⊐<, ∧Ɛ⊐, ∀⊓⌐> ⊐Ɛ⊓∨
>⊓⌐∨ ∨⌐<?

Immediately she crumpled it into a ball. She got up from the table, tossed the paper into the trash, and marched back over to where Lucas was standing. "I thought I told you not to talk to me," she said, trying to sound calm and authoritative.

"But I wasn't. I just thought you might think it was cool. Since you're a Pigpen."

"Since I'm a *what*?"

"Pigpen. I don't mean you personally. I mean—"

"I don't care what you mean. Okay, Lucas?" Zoe said, her voice now squeaking a bit. "Don't call me any names and I won't call you any either!"

"I wasn't calling you a name."

"Oh, yes you were! Don't lie!" This was definitely too loud; out of the corner of her eye she could see people starting to notice them.

Ezra turned around and pulled his earpiece out. "Is Lucas bothering you?" he asked Zoe.

"Yes! But I can handle it." She glared at Lucas, but dropped her voice to almost a whisper. "I didn't just mean no talking, okay? I meant *no contact*. That includes sneaking up on me in the cafeteria and handing me whatever that was. Stupid codes."

He shook his head. "It wasn't a code, Zoe. It was a cipher."

*"What?"*

"Codes substitute words. Ciphers substitute symbols. I gave you a cipher just now. That means—"

"I don't care," she said loudly. "Do you understand? I'm *totally not interested*, okay?"

He opened his mouth to say something. Then he just walked rapidly out of the cafeteria, bumping into a few kids near the exit. They didn't act annoyed, though; they just shrugged and laughed.

Zoe sat back down. She felt terrible for yelling at him in public, but really, what choice did she have? She had to be mean. It was the only way to get through to him. If she even had.

"You all right?" Ezra was asking her.

"Yeah, I guess. That kid Lucas is driving me crazy."

"Me too. Just try to ignore him. Here," he said, and handed her his iPod.

"But it's yours."

"Well, yeah. I'm not *giving* it to you, Zoe. I'll just read my book."

"Thanks," Zoe said uncertainly. She met his eyes, which, she suddenly realized, were grayish green and actually kind of interesting. Cute, even. "Really. That's so nice of you. But I mean, I don't want to use it if you're—"

But Ezra was already lost in his invasion book. So for the rest of lunch Zoe listened to his vaguely menacing hip-hop music, and even though she couldn't make out all the words, she didn't care. In fact, considering the morning she'd just had, she almost enjoyed how it pulsated deafeningly, incomprehensibly, in her ears.

# 12

Finally the day was ending and it was time for Ancient Civs. As soon as Zoe sat down at her whiteboard desk, she groaned.

Because apparently she *hadn't* gotten through to Lucas at lunch. He was obviously the one who'd been writing her tiny messages:

> *4 = Blue.*
> What is 5?
> *Green.*
> What is 6?
> What is 7?

It had to be Lucas. Who else could it be? He probably thought the number-color theory was some kind of secret code she'd invented with her arguable brain damage. Well, maybe he finally understood not to talk to her in the cafeteria, but she wasn't going to let him start sneaking messages onto her desk. Or horning in on her fascinating theory.

So she got out her Signe pen and wrote in slightly larger letters "NOYB!!!" Then she spent the rest of the class doodling on the desk, tuning him out as he interrupted the class with more of his brilliant comments.

Eventually Signe decided class was over, which meant Hubbard was over for the day. Zoe grabbed her backpack.

"One moment, Zoe, dear," Signe said, standing in front of her desk. "May I have a word with you?"

"Oh, sure!" Zoe said hurriedly. "But there's somewhere important I have to be."

"This will be brief." Signe smiled patiently as she waited for the other kids to file out. Then she pulled a grape-colored shawl around her fleshy shoulders. "So, is everything all right with you, my dear?"

Zoe nodded.

"You did not seem intrigued by our discussion today. Is that because the ancient Egyptians have nothing to say to you?"

"I'm sorry. I just couldn't concentrate. I will tomorrow, I promise."

"Hmm," said Signe. She sat down next to Zoe. "So I hear you've been chatting a bit with Lucas Joplin."

"I did. Not anymore."

"Why not?"

"He's a little … strange, isn't he?"

Signe pursed her lips. "In what way?"

"He has this crazy idea about me. And yesterday he followed me after school."

"He followed you?"

"To my afterschool job. Pet sitting." She was about to add *lizards*, but stopped herself in time.

"I see," Signe said. She took off her red plastic glasses and rubbed her eyes, which looked surprisingly small and old. "There are many, many wonderful students at Hubbard," she said slowly, as if she were telling a bedtime story. "But the only person of genius I have ever taught is Lucas Joplin. His verbal decoding skills are truly extra-ordinary." She pronounced the word in the European way: "extra-ordinary," which sounded to Zoe like a contradiction.

"You mean he's good at making up languages?" she asked softly.

Signe nodded. "Encoding, decoding, translating, all of it. When he was five, he mastered Morse code. By his seventh birthday he was reading Egyptian hieroglyphics. Once, he deciphered a code devised by a sixteenth-century Italian diplomat. Nobody could make any sense of it, but Lucas solved it in two months. Of course, none of this is very surprising genetically. His parents are Henry and Eustacia Joplin, both cultural anthropologists specializing in the origins of written languages."

"I'm not … really sure what that means."

Signe smiled. "Well," she remarked lightly, "you either know or you don't know. It means nothing to say you 'aren't really sure.'"

"Okay, then," Zoe said. "I don't know."

"Lovely. Precision is everything, Zoe. Precision and patience. And, of course, intuition."

She put her red glasses back on; now she looked like Signe again. "The Joplins are scholars who travel all over the world studying the texts of ancient civilizations, making comparisons about the early development of written symbols and so forth. Right now they are in Guatemala, observing a team of archeologists at a Mayan dig."

"Whoa," Zoe said, struggling to remember what she could about the Mayans. It was entirely possible that Signe had mentioned them in class sometime when Zoe was doodling on the whiteboard desk.

"Yes, it's all quite exciting," Signe was saying. "These particular archeologists are studying the walls of a buried chamber, and what appears to be an inscription with a rather unusual glyph."

"And Lucas's parents can decipher it?"

"Well, they're not experts in Mayan hieroglyphics," Signe replied. "Very few scholars are. Even the archeologists are stumped on this one, apparently. So the Joplins have e-mailed a sketch of the glyph to Lucas, to see if he can make any sense of it."

"But can he? I thought you just said—"

"Lucas Joplin has a rare talent for reading," Signe said warmly. "If any amateur can figure out this particular symbol, he can."

"Whoa," said Zoe, realizing that this was her second "whoa," and Signe was not likely to put up with a third. "But if he's so amazing, why don't they just bring him along with them?"

Signe sighed. "Oh, they have. They've brought him everywhere, ever since he was a tiny baby. The whole world has been his classroom." She made a large encircling gesture with her left arm, which dislodged her grape-colored shawl. "They'll be back eventually. But for now he's staying with me. I'm proud to say I'm an old family friend."

Zoe considered all this. "You mean," she said finally, "Lucas has never gone to a real school before?"

"That's correct. Hubbard will be quite an adjustment

for him. It's very important that he make a good friend."
Signe stood up abruptly and walked to her desk, where
she began arranging some books. "So tell me, my dear.
How is school going for you otherwise?"

"Okay. I guess."

"You guess? You lack firsthand knowledge?"

"It's fine. Really terrific, in fact."

"Hmm," said Signe. She nudged the books into a small
stack, then looked up at Zoe thoughtfully. "You know,
Hubbard is a very special place. It's not for everybody. I
usually have a strong intuition about these things, but
perhaps it would be better for you to ask yourself."

"Ask myself what?" Zoe said.

Signe smiled kindly. "What you are doing at Hubbard,"
she answered, "with whatever precious gift you have."

# 13

On the walk over to Isaac's, Zoe thought about what Signe had said. (Not the Zoe part; the Lucas part.) So he was some kind of genius crypto-whatchamacallit, apparently. Well, that didn't mean he was right about her; it didn't mean he was right about anything! And if he was so smart about hieroglyphics, if he was so *extra-ordinary*, as Signe had put it, how come he was so dumb when it came to other kids?

Maybe it had something to do with the fact that Hubbard was the first real school he'd ever gone to. *The whole world has been his classroom.* How amazing that sounded, actually. Traveling everywhere with his parents. Assisting on archeological digs. Exploring underground temples. Never having to deal with noisy cafeterias or nasty kids or stupid plays. Hubbard must seem so weird to him. So weird and so, well, little. And he was staying with Signe. How much fun could that possibly be?

Still. Why couldn't he try a bit harder to fit in? Why did he always have to make such a big show about how different and superior he was? And why couldn't he make some other friend and forget about this crazy reading-Zoe business and just leave her alone?

The lizards were hungrier than normal today. Zoe fed them right away, noticing she was starting to run low on crickets. (She'd have to remember to buy some tomorrow, on the way over. The greens were starting to smell a bit weird; she'd have to get some of those, too.) And when she was misting the anoles, she was absolutely sure she heard a few chirps coming from the gecko tanks. Could they possibly be recognizing her? Saying hello in lizard language? That was almost too cool to even think about.

She was starting to love being at Isaac's. It was all so fascinating and calm and orderly. And, except for the occasional chirping, so incredibly *quiet*. The only sort of troubling thing was that Iguana #3 looked a little funny today. Zoe couldn't say why, exactly. But was he (or she or it) a little paler than usual? Were her eyes a little cloudy? And maybe not quite so alert? How was Zoe even supposed to know what she was looking at? She checked what she'd recorded on the chart yesterday: "Iguana #3 took five steps, sat on rock, turned head to left." Not exactly an action-adventure movie, but definitely more energy than now. But what was she supposed to write on the chart? *Iguana # 3 not doing very much. Sitting in corner. Paler?* She imagined Isaac's impatient reaction: *Paler than what?*

She tapped her finger on the glass, but Iguana #3 didn't look at her. Even if Zoe were right about her (and by now Zoe was sure that the reptile looked like a girl), what could she do? Send Isaac another e-mail? Make him leave Arizona and come home?

Maybe Brooklyn wasn't the right place for lizards. Maybe nobody was where they were supposed to be.

The phone rang. Zoe raced down the stairs, hoping it wasn't Deb or Willie. "Hello?" she asked, noticing that her voice squeaked slightly.

"Who *is* this?" A man's voice.

"Zoe, the lizard-sitter. May I ask who's calling, please?"

"Walker Robbins. From the *gallery*?"

"Sorry," Zoe said, wondering if she was supposed to know which gallery the caller meant. "Isaac's not able to come to the phone right now."

"Oh, is that right? Well, tell him there's a major crisis with his biggest wire installation, and the wall's *coming off*. Okay? The wall is literally coming off. And now the insurance company says it refuses to pay, and the opening is in *five days*, and I have *no idea* how to reach him. Do you think,

Zoe-the-lizard-sitter, you can convey all this interesting information?"

"I'll try."

"Well, bless you, my child." Then Walker Robbins hung up.

Zoe ran back upstairs to get her backpack. She took one last look at Iguana #3, who still hadn't moved from the corner of the tank.

"Bye," she said softly. "I'll see you tomorrow. With fresh, yummy crickets, okay?"

She wished she could stroke the small iguana, but she couldn't. The lizards were wonderful to look at, but the thought of touching them still freaked her out. That was okay, though, she told herself. They seemed to like her anyway.

She locked the door and went home.


"Can I ask you a question?" Malcolm was saying as she walked into the living room. "If Isaac numbers his reptiles, and you're thinking about them, Zoe, does that mean that in your head you're actually seeing them as colors?"

"You're just hilarious, Malcolm. I'm practically laughing out loud." She took off her backpack. "Is Izzy home?"

"She's in bed. She said she was tired."

"In the middle of the afternoon?"

Malcolm shrugged. "And Spencer went to the park with Bella, but they'll be back any second. You've been warned."

"Thanks."

Zoe tapped lightly on her bedroom door. Sure enough, her sister was in bed. But she wasn't asleep, because as soon as Zoe stepped inside the room, Isadora groaned.

"Hey! Turn off the light, Zoe!"

"Sorry. You okay, Iz?"

"*No.*"

Zoe sat on the bottom bunk. "Because of the play, right?"

"No, because of the weather! Of course because of the play!" Isadora sat up with surprising energy. "Do you have any idea, Zoe, what it's like to spend all day at school and have to deal with everybody being so *nice* to you all the time?"

"No," said Zoe truthfully. "I don't."

"Well, it's sickening. It's like everybody's thinking, 'Oh, no. Poor Izzy didn't get the lead. Her life is over. Let's hold open the door!'"

"Maybe they aren't sure what else to do."

"Well, I'm not asking them to do anything. It's *my* humiliation. I just wish it wasn't all so public." She moaned and plopped back against her pillows. "Sometimes I'd rather be you, Zo."

"Me?"

"Absolutely. You have the perfect life. You just go to school every day, hang out with Dara, come home…" Her voice trailed off despondently.

"My life is really not so perfect, Izzy."

"How? I mean, no offense, but you have zero pressure. Nobody expects you to be this shining star all the time. And if you mess up, nobody even notices!"

"Oh, yes they do," Zoe said. "Trust me, Isadora."

Isadora rolled onto her side and leaned down. "What does that mean? Is someone giving you a hard time?"

Before Zoe could decide how she wanted to answer that, Isadora added warmly, "You're so incredibly sweet and quiet, Zo. How could anybody be nasty to *you*?"

Zoe winced. "Incredibly sweet and quiet" sounded like "mind-numbingly dull and boring." Not like the kind of person who had fascinating theories about numbers. Or who extraordinary geniuses slipped secret codes to in the middle of the cafeteria.

"It's nothing," she replied lightly. "Just the typical

Hubbard stuff. You remember what it's like in Middle Division, right? And not to change the subject, Iz, but do you think you want some chocolate ice cream?"

Isadora snorted. "Huh? Do I think I want some *what*?"

"Chocolate ice cream. I'm pretty sure there's some in the freezer. I'm not trying to be nice," Zoe added. "And I'm not fetching things either. I just think it might help."

Isadora rolled onto her back. "Fine," she answered. "Go see if there's some of that hot fudge sauce left too."

Zoe scrubbed her hands in the bathroom to get the reptile germs off. Then she went into the kitchen, where Spencer was pulling pots and pans out of the cupboards to construct some kind of obstacle course. And singing loudly:

> *I want a dog*
> *A orange dog*
> *A big, big dog*
> *Because*
> *I want a dog*
> *A orange dog*
> *A big, big dog*
> *Because—*

Zoe opened the freezer. "Can you keep it down, Spence? Izzy has a headache."

"Why?"

"It's hard to explain. People are being nice to her." She found the pint of Häagen-Dazs and hacked out two enormous scoops.

"People are being nice to me, too," Spencer said solemnly.

"Really? Then you deserve some ice cream. If you promise not to sing anymore." She handed him a tiny bowl with about a tablespoon's worth of Chocolate Chocolate Chip. "Here. Don't make a big mess."

"I'm not a big mess. *You're* a big mess."

"Okay, Spence," she said distractedly, studying the ice cream container. *Häagen-Dazs. Strange name,* Zoe thought. It had a secret word inside it: "Agenda." What could you do with the leftover letters? Nothing, really. Hazs. But if you messed up the order, you had "Z's agenda: ha." Which was actually kind of cool, even it made no sense.

"Hey, Zoe," called Bella from the living room. "Want to watch TV with me? Oprah's on."

"No thanks, Bella."

"Just come talk to me, then. About your theory, or your

love life, or whatever else you want. I'll draw your portrait."

"Maybe later."

"Why not now?" Suddenly she was standing in the kitchen, watching Zoe take a jar of hot fudge out of the microwave and pour some over Isadora's ice cream.

"Yum," Bella said, grinning. "Go for it, Zoe!"

"It's not for me. It's for Izzy."

"Oh, really? Why can't she get it herself, then?"

"She can. She just had a bad day."

"Well, so did I," Bella said, opening the freezer. "Perfectly sucky. Is there any of that hot fudge left?"

By the time Zoe returned to the bedroom, her sister was sitting on the bottom bunk.

"Thanks," Isadora said, her eyes actually brightening as she reached for the bowl and spoon. "You know what, Zo? This is the first food I've had all day!"

"Well, that's not very smart." Zoe watched admiringly as her sister twirled her spoon in the hot gooey fudge. Everything Isadora did looked big and important, as if she were performing on Opening Night. Zoe suddenly remembered about Isaac's gallery opening. In a way that was a performance too. Except maybe it couldn't happen if the wall wasn't there. She should definitely tell Isaac right now, she thought. And besides, she'd made a promise to Walker Robbins.

"Um, Izzy? Do you know when Dad will be home? I really need to send an e-mail."

"No idea. Just use my computer, Zo."

"Are you sure? Because Dad told me—"

"Send away," Isadora said, waving her chocolatey spoon like The Queen of Ice Cream.

So Zoe sat down and typed:

> Dear Mr. Wakefield,
>     This guy from your gallery called and said the wall is coming off. He sounded really upset.
>     Very truly yours,
>     Zoe Bennett

She hit the Send key.

"Who are you writing to? Dara?" Isadora asked.

"No. The lizard guy, actually."

Isadora made a face. "Eww. There is absolutely no way I'd ever babysit for a bunch of lizards. I'm pretty sure they give you warts. Or salmonella."

"I don't touch them, Izzy. I just feed them. And take notes."

"Still repulsive," Isadora declared, licking her spoon.

Then she fell back against the pillows. "God. I ate too much. Now I feel sick."

A few seconds later there was a reply to Zoe's e-mail.

> .Hello, Zoe. Stop answering the phone.

She instantly wrote back:

> *Okay, if you say so. I think something's wrong with Iguana #3. I can't tell why exactly, but I'm getting kind of worried.*

And Isaac replied:

> *I don't want to hear your vague inner feelings, kiddo. Just write down # squash chunks and # oz. $H_2O$. I'll deal with this when I get back.*
>
> *Try to be calm and unemotional and just OBSERVE.*

# 14

On Thursday morning Zoe went to school determined to make up with Dara. Not that they'd had an actual fight, she reminded herself. But they hadn't spoken to each other since yesterday morning at the lockers, and Zoe couldn't bear to let things go on like this. She felt hollow inside, as if she hadn't eaten in twenty-four hours and no amount of chocolate ice cream would make her feel like Zoe. Even with everything else on her mind—Isaac's indifference, Owen's threat, the weirdness with Lucas, worry about Iguana #3—the most important thing was finding Dara, talking to her, getting everything back to normal. Or as close to normal as possible.

She hoped she could catch Dara first thing, maybe at the lockers just before homeroom. But when she got there, Dara was standing in front of Leg's locker. So were Paloma and Jake and Mackenzie, and so were Tyler and Calliope. Zoe tried to catch Dara's eye, but Dara seemed too engrossed in something Leg had in her hand.

"Let me see it," Jake was saying. Zoe could see him

snatch a small white strip of paper from Leg. Zoe peeked over his shoulder and read the unnatural, almost-too-perfect handwriting:

> *The next best* [*military operation*] *is to*
> *attack alliances.*
>
> —*Sun Tzu,*
> **The Art of War**

"Okay, it's official," Jake said, half-laughing. "Ezra Blecker has finally lost it."

"How do you know it's Ezra?" Zoe asked.

Everyone turned to look at her. She could feel her cheeks start to burn, but she didn't care.

"You don't know it's Ezra," she said, louder this time. "I mean, do you?"

"We don't know for sure," Paloma snapped. "We haven't done DNA testing or anything."

"Then you really shouldn't accuse him."

"Okay, Zoe. Who do you think is doing this, then?"

"I don't know. It could be anyone, really."

"*Anyone* wouldn't be obsessed with *The Art of War*. Who else reads stuff like that, besides Ezra?"

"Actually," said Tyler, grinning, "that book's kind of

cool. We read it Non-Euro, and sometimes I use it when I'm gaming."

"You read ancient Chinese philosophy when you're playing video games?" Calliope shreiked. She slapped his arm.

"It's not just philosophy. Or just about war. It's kind of like, I don't know, the world's first strategy guide."

"Oh, sure. You're so pathetic, Tyler."

Mackenzie shook her head impatiently. "Maybe Zoe's right," she said. "I mean, about Ezra. Because really, I don't think Ezra even notices anyone else. Has he ever actually spoken to you, Leg?"

"No," Leg admitted. "But who knows what he's thinking in that twisted little brain."

"But you haven't been mean to him lately? Or teased him?"

Leg glared at Mackenzie. "No."

"Are you sure?" Mackenzie continued. "Because sometimes, Leg, you can be slightly—"

"She's never even looked at Ezra," Paloma interrupted. "Mackenzie, you're making it sound like this whole thing is Leg's fault!"

"I'm not," Mackenzie replied firmly. "I'm just saying that if Leg and Ezra never had anything to do with each other, then I don't think Ezra's writing these notes. He has no motive to, okay?"

"So who has one?" Jake demanded. "A motive, I mean."

"Is anyone upset with you?" Mackenzie asked Leg, as if she were now conducting a police investigation.

Zoe glanced at Dara. For the briefest second Dara looked back.

"I don't think so," Leg said.

"Good morning, friends!" Owen's voice boomed. He was walking toward them briskly. "Nowhere you have to be this fine September morning?"

"We'll talk about this at lunch," Mackenzie murmured.

Three and a half hours later Zoe was filling her tray in the cafeteria. She looked at her usual choices—the tuna fish sandwich, the bag of potato chips, the pint of chocolate milk—and she suddenly realized that she couldn't bear to eat any of it. Not one bite. Not even if she were starving. Glancing over her shoulder to make sure no one was watching, she slipped the three familiar items back onto their familiar shelves. Then she helped herself to a large slice of veggie pizza and sat down next to Mackenzie.

Everyone from the morning was at the table, including Dara. Mackenzie was giving a speech about how the perpetrator—that was actually the word she used—had to be someone who had access to the locker area when no one else was around. And since so many kids stayed at school every afternoon and evening for things like play rehearsals and music groups, it probably had to be someone who got to school early in the morning.

"Not necessarily," Jake interrupted. "It's not like you need an hour to stick something into someone's locker. You could do it on your way to a class. Or to the bathroom."

"Then someone would see you," Mackenzie argued.

"Unless the person was a total freak who was never *around* other people," said Paloma, who obviously still thought it was Ezra.

Zoe picked the limp veggies off her pizza and lined them up carefully on her tray. "You know, it doesn't have to be a sixth grader. Maybe it's not even someone in Middle Division."

"Possibly," Mackenzie said skeptically. Suddenly she pointed at Zoe's tray. "What's *that*?"

"It's called pizza. You've never seen pizza before?"

"I mean, what happened to your lunch?"

"The Zoe Special," Jake said, grinning. "Tuna and Lay's."

Zoe shrugged. "I don't know. I guess I got sick of it."

"Just like that?" Mackenzie demanded. "After what? Six years?"

Zoe glanced around the table. Dara was staring at her with a funny look on her face. So was Mackenzie, and so was Leg.

"I wanted something else," Zoe said lightly. "That's okay with you guys, right?"

Then she saw Leg lean over and whisper something into Dara's ear.

Dara shook her head. But for the rest of lunch she didn't look at Zoe once.

That afternoon Zoe stopped off at the pet store for crickets and bought some fresh greens at the corner grocery. All the lizards seemed grateful except for Iguana #3, who didn't eat anything or drink any water, or seem to notice she was there, even though Zoe had sat quietly watching for twenty-five minutes.

Finally Zoe took down the chart and wrote:

> *Bobbed head twice and didn't move off rock.*
> *I'm not sure how to read this but it just*
> *FEELS like something is wrong.*

She thought about Isaac's e-mail yesterday: He'd definitely be annoyed with her for writing about her "feelings."

Well, too bad. She wouldn't erase what she'd just written. Because it was true.

She tapped the glass to say good-bye to the small iguana, carefully replaced the chart on the clipboard, and then walked back home to her own apartment, worried.

# 15

On Friday morning everyone was crowded around Leg's locker, waiting for the next note.

Leg arrived with Paloma just two minutes before the start of homeroom. Leg smiled grimly at everyone, and Zoe noticed that her delicate fingers trembled a little when she opened her locker.

"Nothing," Leg announced, obviously relieved. "No note!"

"Are you sure?" Paloma said. She looked inside Leg's locker, and even felt around the back, just in case the note had slipped behind some books. But finally she was convinced that Ezra-or-whoever had messed up this morning.

Then Paloma opened her own locker. "Omigod. Listen to this!" she shouted. She waited for everyone to gather around her, then read in an outraged voice:

> *There is no greater bane to friendship than adulation, fawning, and flattery.*
> —*Marcus Tullius Cicero,*
> *De Amicitia, XXV*

"What is he, insane?" Leg demanded.

"Let me see that note," Mackenzie said, taking it from Paloma. She studied it, frowning. "Same handwriting. Interesting that it's not from *The Art of War*."

"Who cares *where* it's from, Mackenzie," Paloma snapped. "It just matters *who*."

"Also why," Leg said. Paloma nodded.

Zoe noticed Dara quietly walk over to her own locker and open it. She saw Dara reach inside, pause, and then burst into tears.

Immediately Leg and Paloma swarmed her, but Zoe pushed through. "Dara, what's wrong?" she cried. "Did something—"

"She got a note," Paloma said.

"Dara, you have to let us see it," Leg pleaded. "It could be the same as ours."

"It's not," Dara said shakily.

She handed it to Leg, who read it aloud:

> *Nothing can be more disgraceful than to be*
> *at war with him with whom you have lived*
> *on terms of friendship.*
> > —*Marcus Tullius Cicero*,
> > De Amicitia, XXI
>
> *P.S. The eye of the gecko never blinks.*

As soon as Leg finished, Dara began to sniffle again. Zoe tried to hug her, but she could feel Dara's body stiffen. So she took her arms back, letting them drop stupidly by her sides. Meanwhile her heart was banging in her chest. *Eye of the gecko,* she thought.

"Okay, now this is getting scary," Mackenzie declared. "I think it's definitely time to tell Owen!"

"No," Dara said, wiping her eyes. "I don't want to get anyone in trouble."

"But we aren't. How can we? We don't even know who's doing this!"

"Just forget about Owen. I'm serious, Mackenzie."

Leg and Paloma exchanged disbelieving looks.

"Dara, this could be a real psycho!" Paloma said. "He's not even quoting the Chinese guy anymore. 'Eye of the gecko'—what's up with *that*?"

"I don't want to talk about it, Paloma," Dara said. She shut her locker.

"So what's it doing there, then?" Mackenzie challenged her. "You think it's like a code?"

"A code?" Zoe repeated. "What sort of code?"

"You know. Like if you scramble the letters, or read it backward—"

"Why would you do that?" Zoe asked quickly.

"I bet it's Zoe," Leg suddenly announced.

Zoe gaped at her. "Are you crazy?"

"No, Zoe. Are you?"

Zoe turned to Dara. "You really don't think I'd write something like that, do you?"

"I don't know what I think," Dara replied. "I'm just incredibly . . . upset right now. I'll talk to you later, Zoe, all right?"

"*No.*" She said it much too loudly, but so what. And she didn't care that everyone was staring at them, as if they were performing onstage under a giant spotlight. "We should talk *now*, Dara. In private. *Please.*"

"I can't," Dara said, and then she hurried away.

For the rest of the morning no one talked to Zoe. No one looked at her either. It was the strangest feeling: She didn't want anyone making stupid comments or asking stupid questions, but the fact that nobody was even willing to make eye contact in the hallway was horrible. Scary, even. It was as if some alarm had gone off, silent to Zoe, and now everyone at Hubbard had one single thought: *Zoe Bennett? Anonymous note writer. Even to her best friend: How sick is that? Whatever you do, don't look at her— it could be contagious!*

At lunch she sat next to Ezra, who nodded at her once

and spent the rest of the period reading. Right after lunch was Math. As Zoe walked toward Anya's room, she could see Jake and Mackenzie standing in front of the door, as if they were waiting.

Mackenzie was holding a legal pad and a pencil. "Oh, hello, Zoe," she said somberly, in her police detective voice. "We'd like you to write 'eye of the gecko' on this sheet of paper. Ten different times, please."

"Why should I?"

"So we can do a handwriting analysis," Jake said, folding his arms.

"No, thanks."

"You're refusing?"

"You can't," said Mackenzie, horrified. "If you do, that proves you're guilty!"

"It doesn't prove anything, Mackenzie," Zoe said through her teeth. "Now leave me alone."

She pushed open Anya's door and walked quickly to her seat. She was shaking; she couldn't help it. A handwriting analysis? Whose idea was that? And why did she have to say something as dorky as *No, thanks*? Isadora would have stood up straight and bellowed some dramatic line like *How dare you imply...?* Well, at least she'd refused to take their stupid test. And it wasn't like they could force her to, anyway.

She took her Math binder out of her backpack, and then grabbed a few Prismacolor pencils. *Just for a few minutes,* she promised herself. *Until I can think straight.*

She let her hair fall over her face to form a sort of curtain. And then she began doodling geckoes.

And eyes.

And gecko eyes.

*Everyone is completely blind,* she told herself. They spent all day staring at everybody, but they weren't actually seeing anything. Even Dara couldn't see the real Zoe right now, and how could she possibly fix that? Run up to her at dismissal and shout, *It's me, Zoe! Your best friend, remember? I haven't changed one subatomic bit!* But she knew it wouldn't work; somehow in Dara's eyes she just kept getting smaller and blurrier. Pretty soon Dara wouldn't be able to see her at all.

And then there was Lucas. He saw some things just brilliantly, but he hallucinated the rest. If she tried talking to him, would he even listen? Or would he just call her a brain-damaged pigpen, and then laugh dementedly about her losing her best friend?

Suddenly she felt a hand on her shoulder. "Zoe?" Anya was saying, frowning at Zoe's drawing. "Did you hear what I was just saying to the class?"

"I guess not."

"All right. I'll repeat it, then. Clear everything from your desk. We're having a self-assessment."

"That means a test," Jake called out.

"I don't believe in tests," Anya said patiently. "I just want to see your thought process."

"So why can't we just *tell* you our thought process without having to clear our desks?"

"Will you please relax, Jake? And everybody else: This is a *self*-assessment. That means you guys do the grading, not me."

"It's still being graded," Jake complained.

"Can I hand out the self-assessments?" Paloma asked enthusiastically.

"Thanks, Paloma," Anya said, "but I'll pass them out myself."

"Oh, come on, Anya. Please."

Anya laughed. "You guys are so hyper today! Okay, Paloma, if you really need some exercise, why not." She handed a stack of pale yellow sheets to Paloma, who smilingly went around the room slapping them facedown on everyone's desk.

When she got to Zoe's desk, she slapped down a white sheet.

"What's this?" Zoe asked immediately.

"You heard. Self-assessment," Paloma whispered back.

"If you have a sheet, just get started," Anya called from her desk. "And show all work, please."

Zoe turned over her white sheet.

Someone, obviously Paloma, had written:

$X$ = Anonymous note writer

$Y$ = Loser girl with no feelings

$$\frac{X}{Y} = ???$$

Solve for Zoe.

# 16

Zoe crumpled the white sheet into a tight ball and threw it into the trash. Then she marched up to Anya's desk.

"I need a new sheet," she said.

"Already?" Anya asked, her blue eyes full of concern. "Zoe, I told you, I just want to see your thoughts. I don't care about the computation. Just relax and have fun with it. And if you made a mistake—"

"But I *didn't*," Zoe replied firmly. "Someone else did. May I please just have a new sheet?"

Anya gave her one. She sat back down without looking at anybody, and completed all the problems with fierce concentration, pressing her pencil so hard that she made small indentations in the pale yellow paper.

When Math was over, she headed straight downstairs to the Girl's Locker Room, where Leg, Paloma, and Dara were getting into their shorts and Ts for Rec Arts.

"You think I have no *feelings*?" Zoe demanded. "Is that what you think, Dara?"

Dara's cheeks turned bright pink. "I never said that, Zoe."

"Paloma wrote it, but it's what you think, right?"

"You're yelling. I don't think you want to do this here, do you?" Dara darted her eyes meaningfully in the direction of Leg and Paloma.

"I don't care! And I don't care who hears me! If they want to eavesdrop, let them!" Zoe's legs were shaking; she sat down on a bench. "Listen, Dara. Just because I don't wave my arms around, or dance around onstage, or say every little thing that pops into my head, or *show my thoughts*, doesn't mean that I'm not *feeling* anything. Or *thinking* anything. Don't assume you have me all figured out like some dumb little math equation, because you don't."

"I never said—"

"You think I wrote those notes, don't you? Well, I didn't. I'd never do something like that. To you or anyone. I can't believe you don't know that about me by now. Or that you won't even talk about it."

"Why should she?" Leg said calmly. "When it's so obvious you're lying."

"But I'm not! And I wasn't even speaking to you, Leg. This is actually none of your business."

"Oh, it's definitely my business. I got two notes, Zoe, remember?"

"Well, not from me!"

"From who, then? Your boyfriend?" Paloma said.

"What?"

"Ezra Blecker. You've been eating lunch with him, right?"

"Stop picking on—"

"No, Paloma, I really think it's Zoe," Leg said as she tied her sneakers. "She's the one who's so angry at everybody."

"I'm only angry because you're accusing me," Zoe said. "And you should also stop accusing other people."

Paloma smirked. "Let's get this straight, Zoe. We shouldn't accuse you, but we shouldn't accuse anyone else. Who *should* we accuse, then?"

"I don't know!" Zoe snapped. "Don't ask me to blame other people for you, okay? All I'm saying is, it wasn't me."

"What about the gecko eyes?" Dara asked softly.

Leg gave Dara a questioning look, but Dara was staring at Zoe.

"You're still doing that after-school job, Zoe, right?" Dara asked.

"Well, yes," Zoe admitted. "But that doesn't mean—"

"What job?" Paloma asked.

"Babysitting lizards," Dara said.

Paloma made a throw-up face.

"Listen," Zoe said to Dara. *"I didn't write—"*

"You can say whatever you want," Leg interrupted. "But everybody sees the truth, Zoe. Everybody knows that you can't deal with the fact that Dara isn't your clone anymore. And she got a big starring part and you can't even be happy for her. So why don't you just go off somewhere with Ezra and your disgusting lizards and draw your funny little pictures and leave us alone?"

Zoe turned to Dara, but her best friend was standing there very quietly. Dara didn't even return her look; she just kept chewing on her thumbnail, watching everyone with the same unhappy, slightly out-of-focus expression. What did it mean? What was actually going on in Dara's mind right now? It was impossible to tell; Zoe could suddenly read Dara no better than she could read Lucas's crazy notebook.

Without another word, Zoe got up from the bench and walked over to her own gym locker. She was cold and numb, but her legs were still working. She'd get into her shorts and her T-shirt, and then she'd go into the gym and shoot baskets, or something. And after Rec Arts was Ancient Civs, and then Zoe could escape to Isaac's. And be able to breathe, or cry, or scream, or whatever she wanted.

Her gym locker was in the middle of the locker room. As she walked toward it, she could see that there was a yellow sheet of paper taped to someone's door. Her door. She was positive it was hers. Her heart began to race as she got closer.

In bold red letters someone had written: *Open Me.*

She ripped the paper off the door and let it flutter to the floor. Then she opened her gym locker.

On the bottom shelf was a little white strip of paper, no bigger than a fortune. *Hello, Zoe*, it said. *We know it's you.*

# 17

In Ancient Civs there was another tiny message scrawled in the corner of Zoe's whiteboard desk:

*Zoe, are you there?*

She looked around the room; Lucas wasn't in class. Was he hiding somewhere because he knew that by now she'd read his note to Dara—and figured out that he'd written it, because who else knew that geckoes didn't blink? That's what he'd said outside Isaac's house—she was sure those were his exact words—that day he'd followed her there and sat on the steps and showed her those stupid codes.

She grabbed the Signe pen from her backpack. *No,* she wrote underneath his question. Then she smudged out her answer and wrote,

*Lucas, we need to talk!!!!*
*Urgently!!!!*

After class she grabbed her backpack and raced out the

door to find Lucas. She was just about to run down the central staircase, when she nearly crashed into Owen.

"Hello, old friend," he said.

"Hi," Zoe said, catching her breath. "I was just leaving!"

"I'm glad I caught you, then. Anything you'd like to chat about?"

"Now?"

"We could go into my office. Take a minute. Close the door, talk in private."

"About what?"

"No idea?"

She shook her head. Her hair tumbled stupidly into her face.

"Think about it over the weekend," Owen said pleasantly. "And why don't you stop by my office on Monday morning before homeroom. Oh, and Zoe? You should probably bring a parent."

"What if I'd rather not?"

He raised his eyebrows. Immediately she realized that her question had sounded rude. *Ack! Shut up,* she scolded herself.

"I mean," she added quickly, "is it necessary? To bring a parent? I'm really fine without one."

"Then you're the first kid in history," Owen replied.

• • • •

On the way over to Isaac's, Zoe stopped at a sidewalk grocery for some fresh apples and squash to slice up for the lizards. It occurred to her then that she hadn't eaten anything since breakfast. But she wasn't especially hungry, so she just bought a bag of Skittles, nibbling half the bag before she reached Isaac's brownstone. They tasted comforting, she thought, like normal afternoons. Like *The Zoe and Dara Show,* although she didn't want to think about that right now.

At Isaac's door she stuffed the bag into her hoodie pocket and then headed straight to Iguana #3. And today there was no doubt about it: The little lizard was definitely sick. She was curled up like a teeny cat in the corner of her terrarium. Her eyes looked cloudy and she didn't seem to be moving.

Zoe ran downstairs to the kitchen. Isaac had left the name and address of the vet by his one and only phone. She found it, and was just about to pick up the phone to dial, when it rang alarmingly.

"Zoe-the-lizard-sitter? Is that you again?"

"Yes?"

"It's Walker Robbins. From the *gallery?*" He sighed,

making a loud swishing sound in her ear. "Listen, my child, did you get through to Isaac?"

"I tried. I e-mailed him two days ago."

"Did he answer back? Did he appreciate the seriousness of the situation?"

"Um. I'm not exactly sure."

"Because the wall is totally down now. I mean, I'm standing here looking at . . . air. So if you e-mail him or talk to him in the next, oh, five minutes, could you please convey to him that he needs to get his skinny ponytail on the next flight out of the desert and get home to New York immediately?"

Then he hung up.

Zoe could feel her heart start to pick up speed again. How could she tell Isaac anything? He wouldn't believe her; he'd probably just say that she was reacting emotionally, like some overheated preteen. Meanwhile, the truth was, his perfect little world was a mess, and he was off in the desert somewhere, hiding like a turtle. And leaving her to deal with everything, when she had gigantic problems of her own! Well, she'd e-mail him about the ex-wall later. And of course she'd also e-mail about poor Iguana #3. But she couldn't wait for a reply. She needed to get Iguana #3 to the vet right away. It could be a matter of—

*No. Don't even think that*, she scolded herself. Just concentrate on one thing at a time. Like getting Iguana #3 out of the terrarium. But how was she going to do that? And once she did (assuming she did), how was she going to get the little lizard to the vet?

She needed help, obviously. First she tried her father's cell. No answer, and anyway the Enchanted Forest job was in New Jersey, so there was no way he could get back to New York in time. Mom had patients all afternoon, so it was no use trying her. Isadora had a cell, but if Zoe called, she'd probably just say, *Eww. Warts and salmonella, dahling.* Her only hope was Malcolm. He'd give her a hard time about it, but he'd probably come over, especially if she bowed down and pleaded. She called her home phone number, but it just rang and rang. Then she remembered that this was Friday, and Malcolm always had Math Olympiad meetings on Fridays, which meant he wouldn't be home for at least an hour. And Bella was probably off in the park with Spencer. And even if she wasn't, the thought of dealing with Spencer right now was more than Zoe could handle.

Then she spotted a familiar-looking book on Isaac's counter. The Hubbard directory. Of course he'd have one. His kid Willie was in first grade.

Without stopping to think, she grabbed the directory and looked up Lucas Joplin. As she was dialing, it occurred to her that she was calling Signe's house, but this was an emergency.

"Lucas!" she shouted into the phone. "It's Zoe. I'm at my pet-sitting job. Remember where that was? Can you get over here this minute?"

"What for?" he asked slowly. "I thought you told me—"

"Just come, okay? Please?" She forced herself to breathe. "One of the iguanas looks funny to me, kind of pale and folded up. I think it's really sick."

"So why are you calling me? I'm not a herpetologist. My expertise is in—"

"Codes. I know! But didn't you say there were lizards all over the place in Guatemala, or wherever you were?"

"Well, yes, there were lizards, Zoe. But there weren't iguanas. There were skinks and salamanders—"

"OKAY. Whatever there were, do you think you could please just help me with this?"

He paused thoughtfully. "How? You should probably take it to a vet."

"I'm going to, Lucas. But first I need to get it out of the tank."

"And that's why you're calling me?"

"You're used to them. Didn't you tell me they crawled all over you when you were sleeping?"

"Well, sure. But I never *touched* them. I was asleep. And eventually they crawled off."

"Oh, never mind!" Zoe exploded. "I'll do it myself!"

She slammed the receiver down. What did she expect from crazy Lucas, anyway? Of course, she wasn't done with him yet. There was a whole other conversation they desperately needed to have, about the anonymous notes, among other things. But she couldn't waste time being angry with him right now. Right now she had to save Iguana #3, and who even knew how much time she had.

She ran back upstairs with her backpack. She unzipped it fast, and dumped her binders and crumpled-up doodles and Prismacolor pencils onto the floor. Isaac would probably have been furious about the mess, but who cared? She'd clean it up later. Down the hall from the lizard rooms was a tiny bathroom. She swiped a fluffy white towel from the wall rack and then walked softly into Iguana #3's room.

"Okay, little girl," Zoe crooned, aware she sounded a bit silly, and not caring in the least. "I'm going to take you out very, very gently, and then give you a little ride to the vet in this nice, soft towel. Okay? You trust me? You won't bite or give me bad diseases?"

She clenched her teeth and slowly inched the towel into the terrarium. When she reached the corner where Iguana #3 was huddled, Zoe opened her hand and gently grasped the lizard, who didn't resist at all. Then she slowly pulled her hand out of the terrarium, and carefully dropped the towel-swaddled lizard into her backpack. She zipped it fast, leaving a tiny hole for air.

Then she strapped on her backpack and headed out the door, clutching the vet's address in her hand.

The day was cold, the first real autumn weather of the year. Zoe shivered inside her hoodie, zipping it right up to her throat, and pulling the purple hood over her hair. Probably this was the wrong temperature for lizards, she thought. But didn't it get pretty cold in the tropics at night? Anyway, Iguana #3 was bundled up in the towel. *That should keep her warm,* Zoe told herself, trying to walk as quickly as she could without jostling the backpack. *Which should be squirming,* Zoe thought. Why wasn't it?

Finally she reached the vet's office, almost five blocks from Isaac's brownstone. The receptionist smiled up at her when she walked in the door.

"May I help you?" she asked pleasantly.

"It's an emergency! I'm helping Isaac Wakefield—"

The receptionist immediately got up from her chair and gestured for Zoe to follow her into the back room. A minute later a calm-looking woman with a long brown braid walked in. "You have a lizard? One of Isaac's?"

Zoe nodded. "You're the vet?"

"I'm Dr. Kravitz. Where is it?"

"In my backpack. Could you please take her out? I'm a little—"

Dr. Kravitz smiled. "Sure, no problem."

She walked behind Zoe and unzipped her backpack. Then she pulled out Iguana #3 and carefully placed her on the examining table.

"She won't eat," Zoe said. "And she isn't moving very much. And her color's funny; I can't explain it, exactly."

"Hmm," said Dr. Kravitz. "How long have you noticed this?"

"A few days." She watched as the vet touched the lizard's back. "I don't know anything about lizards," Zoe added. "But I have this definite feeling that something's wrong."

Dr. Kravitz nodded. "Well, it's good you came in, then."

"Then I'm right? You mean she's really sick?"

"Maybe. We'll have to see." Dr. Kravitz crouched down and looked into the lizard's eyes. "What a pretty girl. Which one's this?"

Zoe almost said Iguana #3. But she couldn't. Because suddenly it seemed cruel and wrong that the little lizard didn't have a name.

"Ruby," Zoe replied, wondering where on earth she'd gotten that from.

# 18

Zoe had left all her stuff on Isaac's floor, so before she could go home, she had to go back to his brownstone. It was a long, chilly walk, somehow longer than when she was carrying Ruby, and she was so drained and shaky that her legs felt like rubber bands. All she wanted to do was sit somewhere and maybe close her eyes for a minute and stop thinking about everything. But it was already four thirty, she was freezing, and she couldn't waste any more time.

As she got nearer to Isaac's brownstone, she spotted an unmistakable figure on the front steps. He wasn't sitting all hunched over, but he was wearing that embarrassing tweed overcoat. *Oh, joy,* Zoe thought, balling her hands inside her pockets.

Lucas looked up from his book and grinned at her. "So how's your reptile friend?"

"Not sure," Zoe answered. "Fingers crossed."

"Sorry I couldn't come with you. I was doing extremely important research for my parents. In fact, I cut my afternoon classes to get started. These archeologists have found an ancient Mayan glyph—"

"And you hate touching lizards."

"Right," said Lucas, smiling sheepishly. "Sorry."

Zoe sighed. "Listen, I have to go inside to get my books. You want to come in for a minute and meet everybody?"

He looked alarmed. "You mean the other lizards?"

"Don't worry, they're in tanks. And anyway, it's freezing out."

"That's okay. I'm not even cold. I'll just wait for you here."

"You sure?"

"I never speak if I'm not." He lifted his chin defiantly, but it only made him look like a little kid. Like Spencer, almost. Well, she certainly wasn't going to stand there on the freezing steps arguing with him.

Zoe went upstairs to the iguana room and grabbed her stuff off the floor. Then she peeked out the second-floor window at Lucas. He was sitting all hunched up again, and he was rubbing his arms as if they were numb. Probably with all that traveling he wasn't used to the cold weather, she thought. He'd definitely need a warmer jacket if he was going to make it through the winter.

And then she had a funny thought: *Who would buy it for him? Signe?*

She quickly fed and misted the lizards, not bothering to write down any notes. Then she went back outside and sat down next to Lucas on the rough stone step. "Thanks for waiting," she said softly. For some reason she added, "Want some Skittles?"

"What?"

She took the bag out of her hoodie pocket. "Skittles. I don't know what the name means. The purple are good but the green are the best."

"I know what Skittles are, Zoe."

"Yeah? Well, you can have the rest. I'm not hungry."

"Thanks," he said politely. "Okay if I save them for later?"

She shrugged.

Lucas slipped the bag into the enormous pocket of his overcoat and looked down at the stone steps as if they were suddenly extremely fascinating.

"Listen, Lucas," Zoe said slowly. "I really, really need to talk to you about something. I guess you didn't see the message on my desk?"

"What desk?"

"In Signe's room. You know. The number-color desk."

"What are you talking about?"

"My whiteboard desk. You were just asking me what six was. And seven."

"Seven what?"

She stared at him. "Oh, great. You're pretending you don't know?"

"I'm not pretending anything."

"Never mind," Zoe said tiredly. "If you want to play your baby secret agent games, go ahead. That wasn't what I wanted to talk to you about, anyway." The icy wind was slapping her hair around, so she tucked it impatiently inside her hood. "All right, so here it is: People are getting these weirdo notes. In their lockers. First they thought it was Ezra, and now they think it's me."

"And is it?"

"Of course not, Lucas! It's you. Right?"

Lucas didn't answer. He traced a crack in the step with his index finger.

Zoe watched him. "Why would you do a thing like that? No one's talking to me. They all hate me now."

"So, what do you care? You have nothing in common with them."

"How do you even know that?" Before he could answer, she said, "And don't start telling me I'm brain-damaged, because I don't want to hear it."

He looked up. "I didn't say you were *brain-damaged*, Zoe. I said—"

"Whatever. A crypto-whatever-genius. It doesn't matter, okay? We're not discussing that reading-Zoe business, because it was a totally freak thing. And anyway it's completely irrelevant."

He shrugged. "I didn't mention it, Zoe. You did."

"Well, never mind, then. Forget I brought it up. And I also don't want to hear another stupid word about codes. Or ciphers."

"Fine." He started tracing the crack again.

"Look, Lucas," Zoe said quickly. "What I'm trying to say is, I go to school with these kids. It's hard enough when things are normal, and now they think I'm this crazy anonymous note writer, quoting these—" She waved her arms helplessly. "*Dead* guys. Everyone thinks I'm spying or threatening them with lizards or something, and now they want to analyze my handwriting. And I think somebody told Owen, because he wants to meet with me. And my parents."

Lucas looked up at her. "And then what?"

"What's that supposed to mean?"

"So you meet with Owen. Why does that even matter to you?"

"Why? Because he's looking for an excuse to kick me out!"

"And you want to stay at Hubbard? What for? You don't seem very happy there."

"I'm not. But where would I go? I'm not like you, traveling all over the world. I need an actual *building*—" She stopped and shook her head. How did Lucas keep managing to take over this conversation? She was the one doing all the talking. "Listen, that's not even the point, okay? The point is, why are you doing this to me?"

Lucas folded his arms around his knees. "Those kids aren't your friends, Zoe. They're being nasty to you, they're acting like you're invisible, and you're just sitting there letting it happen."

"That's not true, okay?" She paused. Then she said, "For your information, I yelled at them in the locker room today."

"Really? And how did it go?"

"Not . . . very well." She decided not to mention Dara's reaction, because she could imagine his response: *See? I told you she wasn't your best friend.*

But Lucas wasn't asking for details anyway. He beamed at her. "Well, that's still great, Zoe! You finally stood up for yourself. That's the main thing."

Zoe sighed. "I totally don't understand this, Lucas.

You're happy because I denied writing something that *you* wrote just to get me in trouble?"

"I wasn't trying to get you in trouble, Zoe!"

"Of course you were! That's why you wrote 'eye of the gecko.'"

"No, no! You're completely misinterpreting the whole thing. I was just helping you confront those jerks. And it worked!"

"But it *didn't* work. And I wasn't asking you for help. And what's so great about confronting people all the time? I mean, I don't want to hurt your feelings, Lucas, but everyone kind of hates you at Hubbard."

He tilted his chin at her. "Yeah? Well, so what?"

"You don't even care?"

"Why should I? I'd rather have people respect me, anyway. And at least *I* know who I am."

"What's that supposed ... You think I don't?"

"I think you do know, Zoe. I think you know a lot of things, but then you tell yourself, 'Whoops, never mind, maybe not.' Because you're afraid."

"Afraid of what?"

"Don't ask me," Lucas said. "That's not the kind of thing I know how to solve."

Suddenly he stood up. Then he pulled his embarrassing

overcoat across his skinny chest and walked away, his floppy hair whipping in the freezing wind.

"Zoe? Where were you? You've got like a million messages," called Malcolm from the living room.

Zoe tossed her backpack onto the sofa. "You mean phone messages?"

"Yeah." He was playing Final Fantasy Something, pounding on the controller with his thumbs.

"From who?"

"Don't know," he said, staring at the screen. "It sounded like a few different voices. But every time they just said, 'Zoe, we know it's you,' and hung up."

"Okay. Thanks for telling me."

"You're welcome. Oh, and by the way, Owen called, asking for Mom or Dad. I said they'd fled to Argentina."

"You did?"

"Duh. Of course not." He saved his game, then shut the TV off. "What's going on, Zo?"

"Nothing."

He raised one eyebrow.

"All right. Everything," Zoe admitted. "But I'm too tired to talk about it right now. Maybe later."

She went to her bedroom, where Izzy was sleeping

again, even though it was almost time for supper. Her sister's computer was on, so Zoe opened her own e-mail account. There was one message, but it wasn't from Isaac.

*HEY, LIZARD GIRL. WE KNOW
IT'S YOU SO DON'T DENY IT. IF IT
HAPPENS AGAIN, YOU'LL BE SORRY.
WE'RE WATCHING YOU, AND WE
DON'T BLINK EITHER!!!*

She hit the delete button. She knew she should be using Dad's computer, but under the circumstances she didn't think she could wait for him to get home from work. So she quickly typed:

*Dear Mr. Wakefield,*

    *Iguana #3 was sick, so I brought her to the vet. Don't ask me about squash chunks because I didn't count. I'll tell you what the vet says as soon as I hear anything.*

    *Very truly yours,*

    *Zoe Bennett*

    *P.S. The gallery guy says there isn't any wall now. When are you coming back?*

    *P.P.S. I called her Ruby. She needed a name.*

# 19

Sometime on Saturday, Owen must have called, because on Sunday morning everyone in the Bennett family launched into Be Nice to Zoe mode.

At breakfast Mom made pancakes. This was a big deal because she was definitely not a morning person; as a general rule, it took her two cups of coffee before she could even pour herself a bowl of cereal. But there she was when Zoe walked into the kitchen on Sunday morning, standing at the stove, making Zoe's favorite breakfast.

"It'll be just a minute, sweetheart," she said brightly. "One more stack to go."

Zoe watched her expertly flip the pancakes on the griddle. "Thanks, Mom, but you really didn't have to."

"I know, but I wanted to. Sometimes everybody needs a little extra treat," she said, which just made Zoe's stomach knot up.

Then Malcolm and Isadora walked into the kitchen.

"Pancakes," Malcolm exclaimed enthusiastically. "Can I have some, or are they all just for Zoe?"

"Zoe first," Isadora told him. "You can have the left-overs."

Isadora smiled at Zoe. It wasn't the old radiant look-at-me-I'm-so-gorgeous smile, but it was pretty close. Isadora was really a very, very good actress.

Mom stacked the pancakes on a platter they usually used at Thanksgiving. "Set the table, please," she ordered. "And someone wake up Spencer."

"Not necessary," said Malcolm. "He's been up since five o'clock, barking like a puppy. He says if he can't *have* a dog, he'll *be* one."

"Wow," said Mom, laughing. "That child's coping skills are amazing."

"Yes, they are, Mom. But mine aren't."

Now Dad was in the kitchen, standing in front of the Thanksgiving platter. "Pancakes? All for me?"

"Zoe first," said Mom. "Then Malcolm, then you."

"What about you, Iz?" Dad asked. He poured himself some coffee.

"Oh, I'm off pancakes. I've been eating way too much junk food lately. Not that pancakes are junk," she added, as if she needed to apologize to Zoe.

Soon Spencer came crashing through the door and they all settled down to a loud, happy, sticky breakfast.

Even Isadora forgot about her whole wheat toast and helped herself to a couple of pancakes. But Zoe could barely eat. The breakfast and all the cheery supportiveness obviously meant that everyone thought she was about to get kicked out of school. And sure enough, after all the pancakes were gone, and all the syrupy dishes were dumped into the dishwasher, Mom poured herself a third cup of coffee and said casually, "Zoe? Can Dad and I have a word with you for a minute?"

"Okay," said Zoe, sinking back into her chair.

"We had a quick phone call from Owen last night. He asked us to stop by tomorrow morning before school. Do you know what it's about?"

"Probably."

They looked at her gravely.

"I know I haven't been working very hard," she said quickly. "I *will* work, though. I've just been kind of distracted lately."

"With what?" Dad asked. "You don't mean the lizard-sitting, do you?"

"Of course not!" Zoe said. "And by the way, Dad. Do you know when Isaac's getting back? One of the iguanas is sick and all these people keep calling. I've sent him e-mails—"

"You have? When?"

"On Friday. And the other day. On Izzy's computer."

Dad shook his head. "Zoe, we had an arrangement for all that. You were supposed to use my computer."

"I know. But I couldn't because you weren't home." Before he could answer, Zoe added, "I just needed to give him some urgent phone messages. I won't do it again."

Dad held up his hand like a crossing guard. "That's okay. But never mind about Isaac right now. Let's concentrate on you, Zozo." He gave Mom some invisible signal. "We were actually sort of wondering about *The Zoe and Dara Show*."

"You were? What about it?"

"Zoe," Mom said delicately, "is everything okay between you and Dara?"

"Why do you ask that?"

"I don't know. She's never over here anymore. We don't hear you on the phone. And you haven't been mentioning her."

"She's fine, Mom. Just incredibly busy. She's in the musical. It meets every day after school—"

"We know the rehearsal schedule, sweetheart. We've been through it every year with Izzy." Mom took a sip of her coffee. "So there's nothing else troubling you?

Nothing that if we knew about, we could help explain to Owen tomorrow? Because you know our job is to be your advocates. That means—"

"I know what it means," Zoe broke in. "And I haven't done anything wrong, so there's really nothing to explain." She definitely wasn't ready to go into the whole story about demented Lucas. She pushed a straying curl out of her face.

Mom and Dad looked at each other. Dad shrugged.

"All right, then, ladies," he said, standing up and stretching. "I'm off to the coal mines."

"You're going to work today?" Zoe asked. "But it's Sunday!"

"I know. Not my idea of a good time either. But I just have a couple of minor details to finish, and yet another Enchanted Forest will be complete." He kissed the top of Zoe's head. "And then Monday I start on Lizard World."

Early Monday morning Zoe walked to school with her mother and father. By now they'd given up on the Be Nice to Zoe mode and were just quiet and serious, which was a whole lot easier to take. When they were a block from Hubbard, Mom looked at her watch.

"God, I could really use another coffee," she said to

Dad. "Do you think there's time to run into that Starbucks?"

"Sure," said Dad. "We're supposed to be in Owen's office in fifteen minutes."

"Okay. Then I'll meet you there," said Zoe quickly. She ran the last block to school, even though it made no sense to be in such a hurry.

First she went to her locker to dump her backpack. As soon as she opened the door, she spotted a sealed white envelope on the bottom of the locker. Her heart pounding, she ripped it along the edge.

> *Dear Zoe,*
>
> *I thought about it and I think you're right. Maybe I was trying to get you in trouble because I'm so mad at you. You could possibly have a one-in-a-billion gift for cryptanalysis and you don't even care. But whatever. If you want to be like everybody else, or PRETEND to be like everybody else, that's your business. Anyway, sorry. I won't write those (as you put it) "weirdo notes" anymore.*
>
> *Lucas*

>⊓◻ ⅂◻⅂⊔⅁ ◻◻∧◻⌐
⊔⊢⌐◻⊔∨... ⊔<> ∧⅁◻
◻◻∧◻⌐ ⅁⅂◻◻∨ ⊓◻⌐ ◻<◻∨.

She stared at the letter. Then she read it two more times, and grinned. The code part reminded her of that folded-up note he'd given her that time in the cafeteria, and she refused to know what it meant. But the rest of it was amazingly perfect, like a Get Out of Jail Free card in Monopoly. All she had to do was go upstairs, show this letter to Owen, and then be on her way to homeroom. And if doing that got Lucas in trouble, it wouldn't be *her* fault. Because wasn't she also a victim of the whole anonymous note business? Of course she was!

She slammed her locker door and slipped the letter into her hoodie pocket. Then she ran up the central staircase to Owen's office, taking two steps at a time.

But just before she got to the second-floor landing, she slowed way down.

What exactly would Owen do, she wondered, if she showed him the letter? Probably kick Lucas out instead of her. Which wouldn't be so tragic, really. Lucas could just pack his suitcase and rejoin his parents in some underground temple. *The whole world has been his classroom—*

isn't that what Signe had said? He was used to that; it would feel normal to him. He'd probably even be grateful to get out of this place.

But what if Lucas wanted to go to an actual school for once? It was almost October; if he got kicked out of Hubbard, it would be too late to find him some other weirdo school for sixth grade. And she couldn't imagine him in a regular bells-and-red-pens kind of school, where the kids would probably beat him up just for wearing that horrible tweed overcoat. And then as soon as he started showing off about hieroglyphics and gargoyles.... She didn't even want to think about that.

The truth was, Lucas needed to be at Hubbard, where there were other weirdo kids, and where at least Signe could keep an eye on him. If anyone didn't belong here, it was Zoe, not Lucas. Besides, Dara wasn't even talking to her, so why should she want to stay? And with all the doodling and the missing assignments, Owen had already made up his mind about her anyway. He was just waiting to kick her out, obviously. So what good would it do to get Lucas kicked out too?

By now she was on the third floor, in front of Owen's office. She stepped into the little waiting area, where Mom and Dad were sitting on the tiny sofa. Mom was thoughtfully sipping her paper cup of Starbucks. When she looked up and noticed Zoe, she patted the seat next to her for Zoe to sit down.

"You ready, sweetheart?" she asked quietly.

Zoe nodded.

"We'll be right there with you," Dad said.

"I know."

Mom picked up a copy of *The Hubbard News* from the tadpole-shaped coffee table. "Oh, listen to this," she said brightly. "Remember Izzy's friend Abigail who graduated two years ago? She just had her debut at Carnegie Hall."

"Cool," said Dad. He drummed his fingers.

It suddenly occurred to Zoe that her parents were nervous. *Well, sure they are,* she told herself. *It's not like Isadora or Malcolm ever got them called into someone's office.* For a strange millisecond she actually felt sorry for them. But then she told herself, *No. This is my disaster, not theirs.*

All at once Owen burst into the waiting area. "Good to see you guys," he said warmly, shaking hands with Zoe's parents. Then he ushered them into his office, where there were three metal office chairs pulled up alertly to his desk.

# 20

"So how's Isadora?" Owen asked sympathetically. "I heard she didn't get the lead in the musical this time around. What a shock."

"Izzy's fine," Dad said. "A little disappointed, but that's part of the learning process."

"Yes, it is. Absolutely! I'm a strong believer in exposing our kids to failure. Otherwise, they never truly appreciate success. And there's no doubt Isadora will have a very successful future onstage. If she wants it, of course. Do you know what her plans are post-Hubbard?"

"Not at the moment," Mom replied pointedly. "Right now we're thinking about Zoe."

Owen leaned back in his leather chair and smiled. "All right, then. Zoe. I have to tell you folks, I'm very glad we're having this chat. To put it bluntly, we haven't been seeing a whole lot from Zoe academically, and now I'm hearing some troubling reports from the other kids. Anything you're ready to share with us, Zoe?"

She shook her head. She could feel the corners of Lucas's letter in her hoodie pocket.

"So you're not willing to talk about the anonymous notes?"

"There's nothing to say about them," Zoe said flatly. "They kind of speak for themselves."

"You think so? I know at least a few students who find them fairly cryptic. Some reference to a blinking gecko?"

Dad looked at her sharply.

"I think the note said geckoes *don't* blink," Zoe said. "And I'm not even sure if that's true, frankly."

"Neither am I. I confess I'm a complete herpetological ignoramus." Owen smiled briefly. "And you don't know who *wrote* the notes?"

"It wasn't me."

He studied her face. She tucked her hair behind her ears and waited, her heart pounding.

Finally he leaned forward. "You know," he said, "I've been having some good, long conversations with your teachers these past few days, and we're all wondering what would be best for you, Zoe. Do you have any thoughts on the matter?"

"Not really."

"Ah, but you should. You may remember that one of

Lorna's core beliefs was: 'Every student should actively chart her own educational journey. The teacher provides the compass, but the student creates the map.' Do you know what that means?"

"I think so," Zoe said. "It means don't be a puppet."

"Right. Exactly. So we really do need your input, Zoe. Maybe things will come into better focus if you take some time off for contemplation. We were considering ten days."

*"Ten days?"* Mom cried. "You mean you're suspending Zoe for two weeks of school? On the basis of some ugly, unsubstantiated rumors by two girls who've always been extremely nasty to her?"

Zoe stared at her mother. How much did Mom know, anyway?

"We're not calling this a suspension," Owen said calmly. "It's really more productive to think of it as time to reflect, evaluate, possibly explore some options." He brought his fingertips together as if his hands were holding an invisible crystal ball. "The notes aren't the only issue. It's really the whole picture. And this picture is not what we typically see in a Hubbard student."

"So the problem is I look weird?" Zoe asked softly.

"I actually don't find that funny, Zoe," Owen replied. "But if humor helps you process all this, I understand."

And then he stood up. Mom and Dad stayed behind to have another word with him, and Zoe went to her locker to get her backpack. By now it was almost time for homeroom, and kids were beginning to bang through the hallways, greeting one another ecstatically, as if they hadn't been at school in weeks. A few were gathered in front of someone's locker, chattering excitedly and pointing to something taped to the door.

*It was Lucas's locker,* she realized with a jolt. Pulling her purple hood over her hair so that it almost covered her face, Zoe stood behind the other kids, squinting over their shoulders. The sign was written in a familiar, almost-too-perfect handwriting:

> *ATTENTION:*
> *I WROTE THE NOTES, SO DON'T*
> *BLAME ZOE. SHE'S TOTALLY NORMAL.*
> *SORRY FOR THE INCONVENIENCE.*
> *Lucas Joplin*

Zoe groaned. She didn't know whether to laugh or cry.

*Thanks, Lucas,* she thought. *That was really, really brave. And now you're in gigantic trouble with everyone, just like me.*

*What an incredibly stupid thing to do.*

# 21

The whole walk home from Hubbard, Mom and Dad barely said a word. But when they were back in the apartment, and Zoe was lying on her bottom bunk staring up at Isadora's bedsprings, she could hear them whispering in the kitchen. She couldn't make out what they were saying (and she was pretty sure she didn't want to), but her ears kept straining to catch the words. They all seemed to have S's: "School." "Suspicion." "Decision."

Finally, Mom came into her bedroom and sat on her bed.

"Well, that wasn't much fun, was it," she said gently. "Tell me what you're thinking, baby."

"I'm thinking, Okay, so now what?"

"You don't want to go to Hubbard anymore?"

"Owen doesn't want me there. It's not like I have any choice."

"Oh, Zoe, of course you do," Mom said. "Not *just* yours; the school has to decide too. But Owen really needs to hear what you're thinking. In a way, that's what all this is about." She stroked Zoe's arm thoughtfully. Then she added, "And you know, baby, it's completely fine if you don't want to go back. Hubbard's a great place, but it's not for everybody."

"I know, I *know*, Mom! Everybody keeps saying it all the time!"

"And? So, do you want to go back?"

Zoe looked up at Isadora's bedsprings. They made a fishy sort of pattern. It was funny that she'd never noticed it before. "It's weird," she said at last. "I thought I didn't care. I thought I *wanted* to get kicked out. There's a lot about that place that drives me crazy, actually. But when Owen acted like I didn't belong there, and he said that thing about the 'whole picture,' I got really, really, really—" She considered the perfect word. "Angry," she said.

"Hmm," Mom said, smiling a little. "Sounds like you have plenty to think about. I guess we all do." Then she leaned over and kissed Zoe's hair. "And now if you will excuse me, I have some overbites to correct. Call me later if you get lonely, sweetheart."

And then Mom walked out. There was more whispering in the hallway, but this time the only word she could definitely understand was "Zoe."

She picked up her paperback copy of *The Golden Compass* and stared at a couple of chapters. But her brain refused to focus; the words bled into one another like damp watercolors left in the rain. What else was there to distract her? She didn't feel like doodling. And of course she couldn't call Dara, because Dara was at school. And anyway, it didn't matter, because as soon as Dara saw the call was from Zoe, she probably wouldn't even answer the phone.

*Which is more horrible?* she asked herself. *Getting kicked out of school, or losing your absolute best friend?*

*Losing your absolute best friend.*

Suddenly she realized that Dad was standing in her doorway, holding his sketch pad. "Thought I'd pop over to Isaac's and do some preliminaries for Lizard World," he said casually. "Want to come?"

"You mean now?"

"Why not. You have school or something?"

"*No.* But I'm not supposed to feed the lizards until the afternoon. Isaac said to keep them on a strict schedule."

"Isaac's tough," Dad said, smiling. Then his smile faded. "It was funny about that gecko reference, wasn't it?"

"I didn't write it."

"I know. I'm just saying it was funny." He didn't move.

"Dad," Zoe blurted out. "I know who wrote it. I know who wrote *all* the notes, but I didn't want to get him in trouble. I can't explain the whole thing, but it doesn't even matter anyway, because he confessed. So I'm sure everybody knows the truth by now, including Owen." *Also Dara*, she thought with a strange pang.

"Wow," Dad said, his eyebrows arching in surprise. "Well, that's certainly very good news, Zozo. I'm happy to hear it."

He walked to the bed and reached down and gave her a hug. Then he left too. When she was sure she'd heard the apartment door finally click shut, Zoe got out of bed and walked into the living room. *Two weeks,* she thought. *What am I going to do hanging around here by myself for two weeks?*

She turned on the TV. It was some dumb reality show about a bunch of skinny, nasty people sharing an apartment, but she watched the whole thing anyway. Then she switched over to a science fiction movie, but it wasn't even the kind you could make fun of, so after a while she shut it off.

She yawned. How long had she been sitting there? She checked her watch: something like two hours. At school it was time for lunch. Maybe later in Ancient Civs there'd be another message on her desk. Maybe Lucas would ask her the color for eight.

The phone rang. Who could be calling in the middle of the afternoon? "Hello?"

"Zoe?" someone shouted. "It's Isaac. What are you doing home?"

"Isaac?" she repeated stupidly.

"Yeah. Wakefield. You okay?"

"Oh, yes!" she said. "Totally normal."

"That's good, that's good. Your dad there?"

"He's at your house, actually. He's starting the bedrooms."

"Cool. It's about time. So anyway, I just talked to Kravitz."

"Who?"

"The vet, Zoe. Remember?"

"Oh, right!" Finally she was completely awake. "Is Iguana Number Three okay?"

"Yeah. Just some trouble laying an egg."

Zoe gasped. "She's having a *baby*?"

"Yeah, a cuddly little iguana baby with great big eyes and teeny tiny booties ... No. No baby."

"But didn't you just say—"

"I said an *egg*. Don't get so overheated, kiddo. Sometimes an egg just means an egg." He made a throat-clearing sound. When he spoke again, his voice was definitely gentler. "Lizards do that, you know, lay unfertilized eggs once in awhile. Usually it goes fine, but sometimes they get sick, trying to get that egg out. So then the vet has to help."

"And Dr. Kravitz did? Get it out, I mean?"

"Yeah." Isaac cleared his throat again, as if he were unused to talking this much. "It was good you brought her in. Sometimes you just have to go with your gut, right? Anyway, you were smart not to listen to me. You probably saved her life, and I wanted to say thank you."

"You're welcome," Zoe said, completely amazed.

"But I have to tell you, Ruby's out. How about Winona?"

"Winona? Why *Winona*?"

"I don't know. I just like it, maybe."

Zoe laughed. "Okay, fine. Her name is Winona." Then before she knew what she was doing, she added, "Isaac? You need to come home. There's a lot going on around here. I don't just mean with the lizards."

"Yeah, I know. Walker Robbins tracked me down somehow, and I called Deb back. I just bought my ticket to New York. I'll be home in two days."

"You will be? That's wonderful! I'm so glad!"

"Calm down, kiddo. Just tell your dad for me, okay?"

Then he simply hung up. Zoe stood in the kitchen, grinning. So she hadn't acted like an overheated preteen, after all. Her feeling hadn't been stupid, she'd seen everything the right way, and Isaac knew it. And was grateful! And Ruby/Winona was going to be okay, thanks to her, and all the phone callers were happy, and in two days Isaac would be back in Brooklyn, where he belonged.

*"Hurray, hurray, hurray,"* she sang under her breath. She

spun around the kitchen, then stopped. Spinning was baby stuff; she wasn't Spencer.

Still. This was fantastic! Hubbard was a disaster, but Lizard World—well, *wasn't*. She needed to celebrate, didn't she? Of course.

So she got herself a big bowl of chocolate ice cream, and microwaved some hot fudge.

A few hours later, Dara called.

"Zoe?" she said in a scared-sounding voice. "Are you *expelled*?"

"No! Who told you that?"

"Everybody." She paused. "I'm really sorry I blamed you, Zoe. It was Lucas. He put up a sign."

"Yeah, I know. I saw it this morning. Actually, I suspected him the whole time."

"You did? How did you—?"

"Long story. And the gecko business gave it away."

For a second or two Dara was speechless. "But then why didn't you say something? At the lockers? Or in the gym?"

"So everyone could pounce all over Lucas? Like they did to Ezra? And to me?"

"Sigh," Dara said. "Well, I'm really sorry people were

mean to you, Zoe. It wasn't fair, but you know, everyone was incredibly upset. *I* was upset."

"So was I."

"Well, then, why would you stick up for that obnoxious little—"

"It's complicated."

"How is it complicated?" But Dara didn't wait for a reply. "Oh, great, Zoe. Are you saying you're friends with *Lucas* now?"

"No," Zoe said carefully. "I wouldn't call it that."

"Well, what would you call it?" There was a weird pause. "Do you mean he's like your boyfriend?"

"No, of course not! Don't be crazy, Dara."

Another weird pause. Then Dara sighed. A real sigh, not a word-sigh. "Anyway, whatever he is, you're protecting him, right? And after everything he did at school? I totally don't get you, Zoe."

"Yeah," Zoe said. "I pretty much figured that out."

Zoe hung up the phone.

And that was when she knew, officially knew, that Dara was swimming away. She'd left Zoe behind in the shallow end, and she wasn't coming back. Or maybe Zoe was swimming away; that was another way to look at it. But whichever version you picked, one thing was clear:

They weren't friends anymore. The amazing thing was that Lucas—crazy, hallucinating Lucas—had been right all along.

Her eyes began to sting, but she didn't cry. Instead she went into her bedroom, reached into her hoodie pocket, and took out Lucas's crumpled letter.

# 22

*Dear Zoe,*

*I thought about it and I think you're
right. Maybe I was trying to get you in
trouble because I'm so mad at you. You
could possibly have a one-in-a-billion
gift for cryptanalysis and you don't even
care. But whatever. If you want to be like
everybody else, or PRETEND to be like
everybody else, that's your business.
Anyway, sorry. I won't write those (as
you put it) "weirdo notes" anymore.
Lucas*

>⊓□ ⅂□ᴸⴹᴄ □□∧□⌐
ᴸᴸⴲ□ⴹ∨ . . . ᴸ<> ∧ᴄ□
□□∧□⌐ ᴄ⅂□□∨ ⊓□⌐ □<□∨.

Zoe frowned thoughtfully at the carefully printed
shapes. This was that cipher he'd tried to show her in the

cafeteria; she was sure of it now. It didn't look anything like that stuff in his notebook. But she'd read her name in his notebook. She couldn't explain how or why, but she really had. There was no point denying it anymore. If she tried, if she concentrated really, really hard, could she read her name here, too? And if she could—if her brain was damaged the way Lucas's was damaged, if she could actually do this one-in-a-billion incredibly amazing thing, why was she keeping it locked up inside?

The door banged open. It was Isadora.

"Zoe!" she cried. "Someone told me you got kicked out of school!"

"I didn't," Zoe said firmly. "Big misunderstanding. Listen, I have to do something. If Dad gets back from Isaac's, can you tell him?"

"Tell him what?"

"That I needed to go to Hubbard. I can't explain right now. Sorry!"

Then she stuffed the note back into her pocket and flew out of the apartment.

By the time she got to school, Hubbard was in full after-school mode. Three different singing groups had taken over the lobby, warming up with competing extra-terrestrial syllables ("FWA fwa fwa fwa, fwa fwa FWAAA,"

"SKA ska ska ska, ska ska SKAAA"). As Zoe climbed the stairs to the third floor, some kid ran past her in fencing gear, shouting, "I CAN'T LOCATE MY SABER! TELL THEM TO WAIT!" She couldn't hear the response, just violins screeching and trumpets bleating, and tap shoes clattering in near-precision. The whole building vibrated with a strange, incomprehensible energy. It barely even seemed like school.

Signe's classroom door was open. Still, Zoe knocked on it lightly.

"Come in, whoever-you-are," called Signe's crackly voice.

Zoe stepped inside. Right away she noticed Signe's surprise. For a second Zoe couldn't figure out what she had done that was so shocking. And then she realized: *I'm not supposed to be here. I've been not-exactly-suspended for two weeks.*

"Sorry," Zoe said hurriedly. "I just came back to talk to Lucas a minute. Do you know where he is?"

"Back here," someone called. Zoe looked. There was Lucas, seated behind a laptop. "Be right with you; I'm just logging off," he said, not taking his eyes off the screen.

"Okay." She stuck her hands into her hoodie pocket, and smiled vaguely in Signe's direction.

"We missed you in class today," Signe said.

"I wasn't cutting."

"Yes, I know." Signe cocked her head. "I hope your time off is productive, Zoe dear. But I also believe that time off for sheer contemplation is time well spent. As the great English poet Milton once wrote: 'And Wisdom's self/Oft seeks to sweet retired solitude,/Where with her best nurse Contemplation/She plumes her feathers and lets grow her wings.'"

*Oh no*, Zoe thought frantically. *Now Signe was quoting Milton Somebody at her. Next she'd probably start lecturing about School Suspensions in Ancient History! What could possibly be taking Lucas so long?*

Finally he shut his laptop and stood. "Hi, Zoe," he said brightly, as if he'd just noticed she was there.

"Hi," she said. "Can I talk to you a minute, Lucas? In private?" She said the last two words as softly as possible, because Signe was standing right there, adjusting a paisley shawl. Or maybe pluming her feathers.

"Sure," Lucas said. "Where should we go?"

"I have a wonderful idea," Signe said, nodding slowly, as if she were agreeing with herself. "Why don't you come home with us this afternoon, Zoe. My apartment is just eight blocks from here, and it's a lovely day for a walk."

Zoe looked at Lucas. He shrugged, so she said, "Why not." Which wasn't very polite, probably, but Signe merely smiled.

The walk to Signe's apartment took forever, both because Signe toddled and because she insisted on pointing out the architectural curiosities of every other brownstone. Most of what Signe was saying Zoe already knew, because Dad was equally enthusiastic about the neighborhood, but Zoe was too nervous to say anything. So she just let Signe explain the buildings and kept her head down, every once in a while stealing a glance at Lucas, who seemed to be absorbed in his own fascinating thoughts.

Finally they arrived at Signe's building, a tiny narrow town house the color of rose quartz. Signe led them through an iron gate and up a dim flight of stairs. "Shoes off," she commanded as soon as they reached the only apartment on the second floor. Zoe kicked off her sneakers and lined them up outside the door the way Lucas did, and then followed him inside.

If Zoe had ever imagined Signe living anywhere (and right up to this minute, she really hadn't), this was exactly what she would have come up with: a dark but cozy apartment crammed with books and maps and primitive statuettes and eerie masks and complicated rugs. And if it all seemed a little—to use one of Mom's words—*cluttered*, it was supposed to be, Zoe thought approvingly. It was the home of somebody who considered the whole world her home, who traveled to exotic places, and actually *studied* things, and then shipped home meaningful works of art she'd probably been given as presents.

"Sorry for the mess," Signe was saying. "I wasn't expecting guests today. Although I probably wouldn't have tidied up, anyway. Ask Lucas. He'll tell you what a wretched housekeeper I am."

"It doesn't matter," Lucas insisted. "Nobody cares about that."

"Aren't you sweet," said Signe. "You're the nicest guest I ever had, Lucas. I wish you could stay forever, but alas." She kissed the top of his head. "Well, Zoe, I know you wanted to speak to Lucas *in private*"—she peered over her glasses when she said it—"so I'll be in my library if you need me. And, Lucas, perhaps you can teach Zoe some Pigpen while she's here."

"Some what?" Zoe asked. "Excuse me, but did you say 'Pigpen'?"

Lucas smiled uncomfortably. "It's just the name of a very basic cipher, Zoe. When I called you a Pigpen in the cafeteria, I just meant you were a beginner. But you totally freaked out before I could explain."

"I didn't totally freak out."

"Oh, yes, you did!"

"Well, lovely, then," said Signe, who clearly didn't want any part of this conversation. "Why don't you settle yourselves in the guest room—Lucas's room, I mean. Come and get me if you need anything." She toddled off.

Zoe followed Lucas down the hall to a small denlike room with a massive mahogany desk and a red futon. Lucas went off into another room to get an intricately carved wooden chair, which he brought over to his desk and gestured for Zoe to take. Then he sat in his own much plainer desk chair and looked at her expectantly.

"Um," said Zoe. "Can I ask you a question, Lucas? Does Signe know I read my name?"

"What difference does it make?"

"It doesn't. She said you should teach me that Pigpen code, so I was just wondering."

"Pigpen's a *cipher*, Zoe. Not a code. You need to get that straight."

"Okay. Sorry."

"Stop apologizing! And forget about Signe. Did you get that note I wrote this morning?"

"Yes, actually." She could have told him she'd seen it right before meeting Owen, but suddenly all that seemed irrelevant.

"Well? Could you read the last part?" he was asking.

She pulled it out of her pocket and flattened it on his desk. "That's really what I wanted to talk to you about," she said. "I can't, but I feel as if I could. That probably sounds stupid."

"Not at all." He reached into his desk drawer and took out two red mechanical pencils and a stack of paper. "Okay," he said, grinning. "The Pigpen cipher. Very old, not that interesting, but a good place to start."

Then he hunched over the stack of paper and began drawing four funny-looking grids: two tic-tac-toe boards and two *X*'s. He filled each box with a letter of the alphabet, sometimes adding a dot, sometimes not.

| A | B | C | | J | K | L | | | S | | | | W | |
|---|---|---|---|---|---|---|---|---|---|---|---|---|---|---|
| D | E | F | | M | N | O | | T | | U | | X | | Y |
| G | H | I | | P | Q | R | | | V | | | | Z | |

"*Now* do you get it?" he asked immediately.

"No," Zoe answered, feeling alarmed. "Should I? You haven't even explained it yet."

"Relax. It's very simple." He raked his floppy blond hair out of his eyes. "You encrypt a message by sketching the part of the grid corresponding to the letter." He wrote, "A is ⌐, N is ⊡, S is ∨," and then said, "See?"

Zoe nodded. She grabbed the other pencil and rapidly wrote, in cipher: "MY NAME IS ZOE. I GO TO HUBBARD. I HAVE TWO BROTHERS, ONE SISTER, AND NO DOG."

Lucas glanced at her message. "DO YOU WANT A DOG?" he wrote back without even consulting the grids.

"NO, BECAUSE I DON'T WANT TO WALK IT AND WE LIVE IN AN APT AND MY LITTLE BROTHER WANTS TO CALL IT SIX," Zoe wrote.

"I DON'T UNDERSTAND. REWRITE, PLEASE," Lucas responded in cipher.

"SIX IS ORANGE. REMEMBER THAT WRITING ON MY DESK?" Zoe continued writing.

Lucas crumpled the page and tossed it into a small trash can under his desk. "Enough Pigpen," he said impatiently. "Way too basic. Look at this."

$$6\,V\,B\,T\,H\,T\,Z\,2$$
$$A\,R\,H\,7\,O\,C\,5\,I$$
$$L\,3\,E\,Y\,O\,X\,V\,M$$

"Zoe," she said, after studying it a few seconds. "It says 'Zoe.'"

Lucas smiled. "How did you get that?"

"I don't know. It's just obvious, isn't it?" She pointed to the cipher. "The first space is a six."

"You mean the keyword."

"What?"

"You call that first space the keyword in this sort of cipher. Gives you information."

"Okay, the keyword," Zoe agreed. "So anyway, six means something, right? And if you jump six spaces every time, it spells *Z-O-E*."

Lucas grabbed the paper back. "Do this."

## *IRXUVFRUH DQG VHYHQ BHDUV DJR*

Zoe studied the letters. But this time there wasn't a keyword, nothing to give her a hint what to do. "I'm sorry," she said finally. "I really don't—"

"It's called a Caesar shift," Lucas said. "Invented by Julius Caesar to send during battles. It's just the regular alphabet shifted over three spaces. So *A* becomes *D*, *B* becomes *E*, *C* becomes—"

"Don't tell me," Zoe interrupted. She stared at the letters again.

And then suddenly a strange thing happened. The message just seemed to bloom in front of her eyes, as if it were a big gorgeous flower she had never seen before. "It says 'FOURSCORE AND SEVEN YEARS AGO'!" She beamed at Lucas triumphantly.

"Baby stuff," Lucas said, not smiling now. "We're just warming up. Try this."

He drew another grid. And another. And then a third one that had parts missing. And then a fourth one that was backward *and* had parts missing. And a fifth one with an encrypted keyword. And then five more, each one crazier than the one before.

It didn't matter.

Zoe would stare at the cipher for a minute or two, and somehow it would just burst into sense. A few times she drew a blank, but then Lucas would say something like "transpose" or "multiple keywords." She'd follow his instruction, and then suddenly she would be able to see. Even when he showed her centuries-old military codes from wars she'd never even heard of, or variations of those codes, or variations of those variations, within minutes they seemed brilliantly familiar to her, like a language she'd always known but had forgotten. A dazzling, infinitely sensitive language that you couldn't mess up because it didn't need talking.

She was ecstatic. And very calm, too, somehow, because

everything was finally adding up. *I can do this,* she told herself, over and over, clutching the red mechanical pencil. *It's like this is the deep water, and I'm not even drowning!*

But Lucas, it seemed, was getting tired. He kept yawning; maybe he was bored. "Show me something else," Zoe urged him. "Show me that thing you're working on for those archeologists!"

"You mean the Mayan glyph? Way too hard."

"How do you know? At least let me try."

"No. I mean way too hard for *me*, Zoe."

"Really? But I thought you're, like, this genius."

"I'm not."

"But Signe said—"

He groaned. "I told you to forget about Signe. She's like family, so she's not exactly objective."

"Oh, come on," Zoe said, smiling. "Signe told me you were doing Morse code when you were five years old. You think that's normal?"

He got up from his desk chair and flopped on the futon. For a few seconds he sat there scowling. Finally he crossed his arms and said, "All right, Zoe. I'm good at typical cryptanalysis. That's because I'm good at recognizing patterns. So are you."

"Thanks!"

"But I'm . . . well, faster than you, anyway. So basically I can look at any cipher or code and just kind of read it. Because even though it's supposed to be secret, it's almost always modeled on standard language patterns, you know? But ancient Mayan writing . . ." He shook his head.

"What's wrong with it?"

"Nothing. It's just not a code. It's really more like a private language with its own private patterns. So you can't just pick it up and think, okay, I've seen this before, I know exactly what I'm looking at."

"But why?" Zoe persisted. "I mean, if you're so incredible at reading things, why can't you just figure it out?"

He got up from the futon and started to pace. "Because the system is always changing. I can't describe it. It's, like, I don't know, a kaleidoscope instead of a picture."

Zoe nodded excitedly. "But a kaleidoscope just makes its own patterns, doesn't it? I mean, that's why it's so beautiful."

"So beautiful?" Lucas snorted. "What does beautiful have to do with anything? You don't know a thing about deciphering Mayan."

"I know that, Lucas." She flashed her eyes at him. "But I'm really, really trying to understand. So just re-explain your point."

He sat down again in his desk chair. He picked up his mechanical pencil, clicked it a few times, then put it down. Finally he spoke.

"Those guys were obsessed with numbers, okay? And one single glyph could mean some animal god plus some number he's associated with, even though they also had a completely separate numerical system. Or it could mean King X and Historical Event Y, plus some random verb, like 'to rain' or 'to fish.' Or maybe a phonetic syllable nobody can translate, or a color. And then the colors and shades all mean different things. Like if the agriculture god Chac is written in red, that means east, but if he's white, that means north."

"That's absolutely fascinating!" Zoe exclaimed. "What's south?"

"Yellow, I think."

"And west?"

"Black. Usually. What difference does it make?"

"I don't know," Zoe said. "I'm just curious. Can I at least see this glyph?"

"Whatever," Lucas said. He got up from his desk and came back a minute later with his laptop. Then he logged on to to his e-mail and opened an attachment. Instantly a smudgy charcoal drawing filled the screen: a flat, shadowless profile of a bird-woman or bird-man, it was impossible to tell which. But whatever it was had long, flowing hair. And a hawk's beak and a big stomach with four perfectly round dots lined up in a horizontal row. And an eye that was unusually large—not scary, really, but just kind of watchful. Almost like a lizard's eye, but not like one she recognized from Isaac's.

Still, she was positive she'd seen this creature before. *Oh, right,* she thought. *The spiral notebook. Those weird drawings in the back.*

"Whoa," she said softly. "It's amazing, Lucas. And you're supposed to decipher it? I wouldn't even know where to begin."

"No, you wouldn't. The standard strategy would be to compare it detail by detail to other known glyphs. But as far as I can tell, this one is completely unique. Freakish," he added, glancing quickly at Zoe.

She pretended not to notice. "Then how can you know what you're even looking at?"

"Right. Exactly. I've been trying to research it electronically, but I'm not getting anywhere. And the Hubbard library sucks, to be honest. So I've been drawing it a lot, hoping maybe that'll trigger something. But really, the only way to decipher it would be to see it in context."

"In context? You mean like going to Guatemala?"

"Yeah. I don't know what I'm doing here, anyway."

"Lucas," Zoe said impulsively. "Why exactly *are* you here?"

He shrugged. "Signe convinced my parents that I should try a real school for a little while. As an experiment."

"And . . . what do you think?"

"I think it's been a rousing success, don't you?"

"Yeah, well." She tried to smile encouragingly. "Maybe you need to give it a little more time."

"Maybe," Lucas said. "But Owen knows I sent the notes, so who knows how much time I'll even have. He's put me on probation. He says if I commit any other 'offense against the Hubbard community,' I'm out."

"But can't Signe talk to him? And explain how you were just trying to help me? And how you didn't know how to act because you never went to school before—?"

"She's not omnipotent, Zoe. Even if she thinks she is." Lucas stood up and stretched. "Are you hungry? Signe's a terrible cook, but she can manage spaghetti."

Zoe glanced at her watch. It was six thirty-five. She hadn't fed the lizards yet. And her parents had no idea where she was. "Thanks, but I have to go. Can I have one of those pictures you drew?"

"You mean of the glyph? What for?"

"Just to have. Something to think about the next two weeks."

"You're not going to solve it, Zoe."

"Oh, I know that."

He opened his desk drawer and took out his little spiral notebook. Then he ripped out a page from the back and handed it to her.

"Thanks a *lot*," Zoe said sincerely. "And for the cipher lesson. And everything else."

He grinned. "No perspiration," he said, which was such a demented thing to say that it made Zoe laugh out loud.

# 23

The next two weeks flew by. Every morning Zoe took the subway with Mom to Grand Army Plaza, to the main branch of the Brooklyn Public Library. (Zoe had argued that she was old enough to take the train by herself, but she was secretly relieved that Mom had insisted they go together.) Mom's orthodontist office was just a few blocks away, so after a long morning of exploring the shelves in the Codes and Ciphers section, Zoe would meet her for lunch at one of the nearby cafés. Mom didn't really understand what Zoe was researching, but she asked a lot of smart questions that showed she was interested. And she always let Zoe order something gooey for dessert, even though, according to her, it was nothing but fat and cavities.

After lunch Zoe would return to the library and focus on pre-Columbian civilizations. She took down book after book about the Mayans, scribbling down all the notes she could. She even surfed the Internet, Googling "glyphs" and "Mayan writing" and then, finally, desperately, "Guatemalan temples."

Lucas was right, she quickly realized. The Mayans were completely crazy. They were obsessed with writing, apparently, but they clearly hated reading. How else could you explain the hundreds of glyphs that meant a bunch of different things depending on—well, who knew what. But it was just as Lucas had told her: One simple Mayan glyph could mean five different things. Or just one thing. Or not even a *thing*: just a sound, sometimes.

Plus, deciphering the glyph wasn't like sitting in Signe's guest room and staring at one of Lucas's ciphers, which all of a sudden, if you transposed a few letters, or messed with the keyword, you could comprehend. Because with the Mayans every boxy little glyph was crammed with private symbols, private meaning: mythology and history and mathematics and religion, all tangled up with strange and gorgeous geometric designs, and jaguar heads and snakes. And unless you were a Maya scholar, or an archeologist, or whatever kind of symbol-comparing expert Lucas's parents were supposed to be—unless you had some sort of magical key that would let you unlock the whole complicated, mysterious world packed into that private language, you couldn't possibly just spend a few afternoons in the library and have the faintest clue what you were looking at. You couldn't will yourself to understand, even if you had some gift or brain damage or whatever it was that let you read your name on a page of Lucas's notebook.

And of course, Zoe reminded herself, Lucas's glyph was a freak—it wasn't even like the *known* glyphs. So if the regular ones were impossible to read, then this one was—well, what? A kind of sick Mayan joke?

But whatever it was, she refused to give up. She sat in the library until her eyes hurt and her back ached, taking so many notes that by the end of the day her fingers felt like claws. And then at precisely five o'clock, Bella and Spencer would meet her outside the library to take the train, Spencer shouting "CHOO-CHOO-CHOO" the entire ride home.

Once Bella asked her what she was working on.

"Everything," Zoe replied tiredly. "Ciphers and codes in general, one ancient Mayan glyph in particular. But I'm not getting anywhere."

"You're amazing, Zoe," Bella said as she grabbed Spencer's hand out of her backpack. "I mean, your whole family is amazing, but you're the coolest one."

"I am?"

"Oh, definitely. I've always thought so. I mean, Izzy and Malcolm are great, I love them both. But they're so out there, you know? It's like, 'Look at me, look at me' all the time! And don't even get me started on you-know-who," she added, rolling her eyes in the direction of Spencer.

Zoe had to smile at that.

"Anyway, you're different," Bella continued. "You're so private; I didn't really notice you at first. But I mean, that whole color theory of yours, and now this code stuff. Spence, I said *no lipstick*." She snatched it away before he could draw on the train seat.

"The color theory is completely separate," Zoe said softly. "It has nothing to do with deciphering glyphs."

"Well, whatever it has to do with, I just think it's very cool."

"Thanks, Bella." Zoe looked out the train window at the blurry rooftops. If you squinted, they all ran together in a kind of medium-grayish purple. A nice, peaceful kind of color that didn't really have a name. Or a number. Or maybe it did but her brain was just too jumbled and exhausted to think of it.

When she got home, she dumped her notes onto her desk and then went over to Isaac's. By now Isaac was back in Brooklyn, but he was spending so much time at the gallery fixing his wire installation that Zoe just kept the regular feeding and watering schedule. She still loved it at his brownstone, and she was attached to the lizards, especially the shy golden gecko and Ruby/Winona, safely back from the vet. Besides, Dad was over there every day painting the bedroom walls, and she loved seeing the way he made the deserts and savannas and woodlands bloom, inch by exotic inch.

One late afternoon, about a week and a half into her not-exactly-suspension, Dad finished a particularly tricky bit of vegetation and then put down his paintbrush. "So, Zozo," he said. "I had a phone call from Owen today."

"Owen?"

"Remember him? Remember school?"

"Of course I do! What did he say?"

"Well, the first part was a question. He wanted to know if you intended to come back."

"To Hubbard?"

Dad smiled patiently. "Have you given it any thought?"

Here was the funny thing: For the past week and a half, she hadn't. She'd just assumed she was going back. That's why she hadn't called Lucas. She wanted to walk into the building after two weeks of glyph research and report to him what she'd found. Or hadn't found (which seemed likelier). It never even occurred to her that she wouldn't return to see him in the cafeteria, or at least in Ancient Civs. Because if Lucas belonged at Hubbard, well, obviously so did she.

"I want to go back," she answered. Then she added, "If they'll let me."

"Yes, well, that's where it gets interesting."

"What do you mean?"

"You've been put on academic probation. That means unless you start working and stop doodling, you're out."

Zoe nodded. Lucas was on probation too. A different kind, a don't-write-anonymous-notes-or-else kind. But now they were both just hanging on by their fingertips, it seemed. "Okay," she said solemnly.

Dad wiped off his hands on a paint-spattered rag. "You're really lucky," he said. "From what I could gather, it sounded like the main reason you've been given another chance is that Signe stepped up for you."

*"Signe?"*

"She offered to be your special faculty adviser. You're going to have to talk to her about schoolwork on a daily basis. Think you can handle that, Zo?"

"I guess. I mean, I'll try to, Dad."

"I know you can," he replied seriously, putting his

hands on her shoulders. Then he winked at her. "And they expect you back on Monday."

"Monday?"

*Three days,* she told herself.

From then on she spent every minute she could at the library, not even taking a break on the weekend. But she wasn't researching the whole time. Now she was also drawing the glyph over and over, just the way Lucas had in his little spiral notebook. And the amazing thing was, every time she drew it, she saw the color blue. This was very strange, because she was using a normal lead pencil, and the actual glyph had been written in black charcoal. *So where did blue come from?* she wondered. *Why blue?*

It was Sunday night, and she was lying in her bottom bunk staring up at Isadora's bedsprings when it finally occurred to her: *Blue because of the four dots. Blue because 4 = Blue.*

She immediately told herself she was being stupid. The number-color thing was her own personal theory. It was just the way she saw things, like a kind of mental doodling. Really, it was only a feeling; it wasn't anything she could ever prove or could even use. So it couldn't have anything to do with deciphering the weird, impossible language of some ancient civilization. Because it had nothing to do with reality. It had nothing to do with anything. It was just Zoe being . . . Zoe.

She huddled under her blanket and shut her eyes tight. But that night the color blue was so brilliant and beautiful that she never fell completely asleep.

# 24

On Monday morning Isadora and Malcolm walked Zoe back to school. They didn't make a big thing out of it. They just waited for her to brush her teeth and then casually picked up their backpacks and followed her out of the apartment. Isadora was in an especially good mood, having decided, as of Friday afternoon, to assistant stage-manage the musical. "It's incredibly fascinating," she chattered happily. "Maybe even more fun than performing. Okay, not *more* fun, but close. And to tell you the truth, Zoe, I didn't realize it, but I was practically starving for a challenge!" Meanwhile, Malcolm was going on and on about how many points he'd scored in the last Math Olympiad, but Zoe was only half-listening, anyway. Mostly she was thinking about what she was about to tell Lucas, and what, if anything, she would say to everybody else.

As soon as she got to her locker, Mackenzie rushed to her side.

"Welcome back," she said, as if she owned the school. But she was smiling so sweetly that Zoe had to smile back.

"Are you mad at me, Zoe?" she asked. "I feel absolutely horrible."

"It wasn't your fault, Mackenzie."

"I know. But I blamed you for the notes. And then I asked you for your handwriting."

"It's okay."

"But it wasn't," Mackenzie insisted. "You should be furious with me. You should be furious with everybody! Especially Lucas."

"Oh, no, don't blame Lucas."

"Why not?"

"Because he's a really nice person. And people are so nasty to him. Not you," Zoe added, noticing she'd offended Mackenzie. "Other people."

"Yes, well," Mackenzie replied. "Maybe if he was nicer to other people, they wouldn't be so nasty to *him*."

"I know, I know. He really messed up. But just give him another chance, okay?" Zoe closed her locker. "I'm supposed to see Signe before homeroom. I'd better run."

"Good luck," Mackenzie said. "Oh, and Zoe? Can I give you some advice? Look her right in the eye and speak loudly. She likes that."

"Okay. Thanks." Then she smiled. If anyone had told Zoe three weeks ago that she'd be taking Signe-advice from Mackenzie Stafford, she'd have thought they were crazy.

She climbed the stairs to the third floor, not even minding the typical Monday morning crush of kids with their French horns and lacrosse sticks and earsplitting hellos. Then she knocked on Signe's door. No answer. "Hello," she called loudly, and waited for a response, but nothing happened. So she walked inside the classroom.

What she saw made her gasp.

There was Lucas, wearing his hideous brown overcoat. He was standing in the back of the room holding two enormous suitcases.

Suddenly he beamed at her. "Hey, Zoe. You made it just in time!"

"For what?"

"The taxi's coming. You almost missed me."

"What are you talking about?"

"I'm leaving for the airport. Signe just called a taxi."

She stared at him. "Why are you going to the airport?"

"Because you can't walk to Guatemala."

"You mean you're leaving Hubbard?" she asked stupidly. "Right now?"

He shrugged.

"But you can't, Lucas! What about school?"

"It was only an experiment, remember? And I finally convinced my parents that it failed."

"But it didn't," she said quickly. "I mean, you *didn't* fail. You're just on probation. So what? So am I!"

"It's not the probation. I just don't belong here, Zoe. Don't tell me you didn't know that." He tilted his chin at her in that defiant way of his.

"But you've only been here a month. It'll get better."

"Maybe."

"Look, I'm sorry I said people hated you. They don't. They just don't know you yet. I only said it because I was angry."

He shook his head impatiently. "It doesn't matter. I really do need to be in Guatemala. The archeologists are holding this major press conference in two weeks. I've convinced them that the glyph may possibly predate every other Mayan glyph ever discovered."

"What do you mean—"

"I think that the reason we couldn't decipher it is that it's from an earlier writing system. Maybe *much* earlier."

He waited for a reaction. When she didn't say anything, he added, "And that could mean the Maya developed hieroglyphics centuries before anyone supposed!"

Her brain was struggling to keep up with the conversation, which seemed to be happening too fast for her right now. She had to say something, clearly, but it was hard to think of what. Then she saw that his eyes were shining, so she said, "Whoa. That's really amazing, Lucas. But how did you figure that out?"

He grinned. "By looking. After you left Signe's apartment, I stayed up the whole night just studying the glyph, comparing it to others. The headdress was funny—kind of fatter, didn't you think? And the eye: Did you notice the way it kind of stared at you? No other glyph has an eye like that—at least, not any I've ever seen. So then I thought: Maybe the glyph wasn't impossible to read; maybe it was just different. And then I thought: Well, why would it be different? Was it from another time? And I e-mailed my parents, and they showed it to the archeologists, who agreed that was a possibility. So they're flying in these other archeologists to run radiocarbon tests on the charcoal. That'll help them date the glyph, which could be the first step toward deciphering it. Anyway, I asked my parents if I could come watch, and at first they were against it. But then Signe got on the phone and stuck up for me, and they said yes."

"Whoa," Zoe repeated. "And then you'll be famous."

"No, I won't. And who even cares about that?"

"I know. I'm just saying." *Shut up,* she yelled at herself.

"But after all that, I mean after the tests and everything, you could come back to Hubbard, right?"

"Theoretically. But only to visit Signe. And you, if you're not too mad at me."

"I'm not mad," Zoe said. But it was a lie. She wasn't mad at Mackenzie, but she was incredibly mad at Lucas. Because how could he just fly off like this? And not even warn her ahead of time? Did he think she wouldn't care if he was gone from school by the time she came back?

And who was she supposed to be friends with now? Lucas was the only one she had anything in common with. He'd said so himself that first time they'd argued in front of Isaac's brownstone, and then again when they'd sat freezing on Isaac's steps. And now he was acting as if the whole reading-Zoe thing had never happened. Or the notes. Or that afternoon at Signe's. It felt almost as if he, too, were swimming away, leaving her to—what, exactly? The shallow water? But she didn't even belong there anymore.

He checked his watch. "I need to meet Signe in the lobby. You want to come?"

Zoe nodded helplessly. They ran into Signe just as they entered the staircase.

"So you're ready?" Signe asked, panting a little. "Oh, hello, Zoe dear. Lucas has a farewell party, I see."

"It's not a farewell party. I didn't even know he was leaving," Zoe murmured.

"Well, neither did I, and neither did he! We just arranged it all last night. Everything's happened so quickly." Signe took off her red plastic glasses and rubbed the lenses on her coral pink scarf. Her white bun was loose and sliding down to her left ear; she looked exhausted. "Zoe, grab a suitcase, please. I'm afraid my old back forbids carrying luggage."

"So you're coming to the airport?" Lucas asked Signe excitedly. "Don't you have classes to teach?"

"I'm sure my students will survive a day off," Signe said dryly. "Now hurry, both of you. The taxi driver called my mobile. He's on his way to the school."

Zoe gripped the handle of a beat-up-looking, mouse-gray suitcase that had probably accompanied the Joplins all over the world. For a second she imagined that it was her suitcase, that she was flying off with Lucas to some mysterious Mayan temple, and a team of eager archeologists would greet her when she landed. But of course that was just silly. She'd probably never get to do anything that extraordinary in her entire life.

It was beginning to drizzle on the street, so Signe suggested they wait for the taxi inside the Hubbard lobby. Lucas immediately started to pace in front of the interior swinging doors, but then he stopped abruptly and reached inside his coat pocket for his little spiral notebook.

"Just checking to make sure I had it," he said, smiling sheepishly.

And that's when Zoe remembered why she'd needed to talk to him, or at least had thought she did. It all seemed kind of ridiculous now, but she knew if she didn't speak up, she'd never forgive herself. Glancing quickly at Signe, who was poking her head out the front door, Zoe walked over to Lucas and touched him lightly on the arm.

"Listen," she said quietly, hoping Signe couldn't hear what she was about to say. "You're going to think this is strange. Or demented, or something, but I have to tell you: *four blue.*"

"Four blue what?"

"I don't know," she admitted. "I was drawing the glyph over and over, just like you did. And—" She stopped.

"And what?"

"I have this theory about numbers. I mean, I see them as colors; I always have. That's what I was writing on my whiteboard desk. Anyway, every time I drew the four dots on the glyph, I saw blue. Because four *is* blue."

"I see the taxi," Signe announced. "Let's move outside, shall we."

A shiny black Town Car—not what Zoe considered a taxi at all—pulled up to the school entrance. The driver opened the trunk and tossed in the two suitcases, clearly unimpressed with their appearance.

"JFK?" he barked.

"That would be lovely," Signe replied, as if he'd just asked her to dance.

She allowed the driver to open the door for her, and then stepped in gracefully, as if she were wearing glass slippers and not high-top sneakers with NBA logos. Lucas followed awkwardly, his skinny legs arriving in the seat a couple of seconds after he did. It occurred to Zoe then that this was it, Lucas Joplin was really leaving. She couldn't talk; there were words in her throat, but her mouth just wasn't working anymore.

He rolled down the window and grinned at her. "Four blue," he said. "Okay, you're right, Zoe: That really *is* demented. I think you've been spending too much time with the lizards."

She shook her head and grinned back at him.

*Four blue,* she told herself as the car sped away. *No, it isn't demented, Lucas. Four blue.*

# 25

For the next few weeks Zoe was the perfect Hubbard student. She turned in all her assignments on time and didn't doodle once during class. She even raised her hand every once in a while to ask smart questions that proved she was paying attention. Signe was pleased with her; she told Zoe so every day when they met in the morning before homeroom. And after a week or so Owen called Mom and Dad to tell them "things seem to be on track," which made Zoe feel like one of Spencer's train sets that had been rescued after derailing.

At lunch Zoe sat with Ezra at the weirdo table. Sometimes Mackenzie and Jake joined them, challenging each other to remember song lyrics and lines from movies, but mostly they were okay, and Zoe could tell Ezra enjoyed the company. (He even put away his iPod most of the time.) Every once in a while she spotted Dara at a far-off table, but Dara never seemed to look up at the precise moment Zoe was watching her, and she probably thought Zoe had forgotten all about her. Or maybe Dara had forgotten all about Zoe. That was actually way more likely.

Mostly, though, Zoe thought about Lucas. She wondered if he was happy being back with his parents, or if he missed anything at all about going to Hubbard. And she wondered if she'd ever find out what had happened with the glyph dating. Because even if a super-ancient hieroglyph was big news to archeologists, it probably wasn't the sort of story that would make the local papers. Maybe she could Google "Mayan writing" or even "Lucas Joplin" and see if the story had been picked up anywhere.

Or possibly she could just ask Signe, who seemed to know everything that was going on with the Joplin family. But she imagined herself meeting Signe before homeroom and saying something like, *I did my Do Nows for Anya and I wrote an essay for Babe-riel and, oh, by the way, has Lucas e-mailed you anything about four blue something-or-other?* And then she imagined Signe's amused-but-uncomprehending reply. *You like pizza? I have a feeling you will change dramatically.*

Probably, Zoe told herself, she'd never hear from Lucas again, about the glyph or anything else. Probably he'd never come back to Hubbard, even for a visit.

And then one day as she was taking her seat in Ancient Civilizations, she noticed something on her whiteboard desk. In the lower left-hand corner there was a tiny message written in smudgy purple marker:

> Hello, Zoe. Long time no write.
> What is 12?
> What is 13?

She gasped so loudly that Mackenzie cried out, "Zoe? Are you okay?"

"Fine," she answered, turning crimson. She could hear Leg and Paloma giggling as Signe swept into the room.

"Zoe, I'd like to chat with you after class," Signe announced. "That is, if you don't have other plans."

For a second Zoe thought Signe had to be kidding. What other plans could she have that were more important than the return of Lucas Joplin—because how else could you decipher the smudgy message? He'd told her he hadn't been the one writing on her desk, but obviously he'd just been playing dumb. Because if it wasn't Lucas, who else could it possibly be?

"Sure," she managed to say. Signe nodded, and then the lesson began, something about Mesopotamia that Zoe was too distracted to even hear.

At last class was over. Zoe stayed seated until everyone

else had left the room (including Mackenzie, who had come rushing over to Zoe's desk to ask if she was absolutely sure she was all right). By the time Signe closed the door and toddled back to her desk, Zoe could barely keep herself from shouting, "Then he's back?"

"Who, dear?"

"Lucas Joplin!"

"Why, no. He's in Guatemala. As you're well aware."

Then who'd written on her desk? Zoe stared blindly at the smeary handwriting.

"*You* wrote on my desk, didn't you?" she said finally. "It was you the whole time."

"Oh, no," Signe said, smiling playfully. "So I've been discovered at last."

"But—that's graffiti!"

"No, my dear, it isn't. Graffiti is a permanent ugly scar; I abhor graffiti, despite its origins in Ancient Rome. Did you know, Zoe, that graffiti is derived from the Italian '*graffiare*,' meaning 'to scratch'? Originally graffiti was carved into walls, sort of the opposite of hieroglyphs, which were *sacred* carvings."

Signe swiped her hand through the purple message; instantly, it appeared on her fingertips. She beamed at the shiny white desktop. "Aren't these whiteboard desks just marvelous? I knew they inspired good listening skills, but I'm also convinced they stimulate communication."

Zoe stared at her teacher in shock. "I thought I was writing to Lucas."

"Yes, I realized that. And that's why I stopped."

"But why did you—"

Signe sat herself at the desk closest to Zoe's. She lined up her purple fingertips as if she were praying to some crazy ancient god. "Every once in a while," she said, as if she were telling another bedtime story, "there's a student you simply cannot figure out. You can tell she's very bright, a creative thinker, potentially, and yet she remains something of an enigma. And so you try everything you can think of—special games you can share, projects perhaps. Anything that could spark some kind of connection."

"And that's what you were doing? Playing games with me?"

"No, of course not, Zoe. Please just listen for a moment." Signe removed her red plastic glasses and perched them carelessly on top of her head. "I could see you were terribly uncomfortable in my classroom, my dear. But you were very engrossed in your whiteboard, so one day I had a little peek. And when I saw this equation you were making between numbers and colors, it suggested to me that you had the sort of unconventional but systematic mind I've always found so intriguing."

Zoe couldn't believe her ears. So Lucas hadn't been pretending. He really hadn't had a clue about the number-color desk. And meanwhile, all this time, it had been her own teacher—the scariest person she knew—who'd been sending her secret messages about her theory. Which she obviously thought was fascinating. Or anyway, not totally brain-dead.

"Okay," Zoe said uncertainly. "But then why did you write on my desk just now?"

"Only to continue our conversation. Because I don't want you to think nobody's interested. Even if Lucas *isn't* around."

She patted Zoe's arm. Then she toddled over to her desk and opened the top drawer, taking out what looked like a small tube of paper, fastened with a rubber band.

"Here," she said, walking back and handing it to Zoe. "This arrived yesterday in a package the Joplins sent to me. It's from Lucas. He said he thought you might like to see it."

"What is it?"

"Well, if that's truly a question, Zoe dear, why don't you have a look?"

Zoe slid off the rubber band and unrolled the tube. On the top was a note from Lucas, written in Pigpen: "Hi, Zoe. Guatemala is really cool, despite the lizards, which I still refuse to touch. Oh, btw. Did you know Texas banded geckoes have moveable eyelids? That means they can blink. So disregard everything I ever said. Lucas. P.S. Thought you might like deciphering these pages. Let me know if you're stuck."

The second sheet of paper, and the third, and the fourth, she recognized instantly: the Zoe cipher. The spiral notebook pages he'd written in the lunchroom that first day at Hubbard. She stared at the strange symbols. Maybe she was ready to read the whole thing now. Maybe not. "Thanks, Signe," she said softly. She rolled up the tiny pages again and slipped them into her pocket.

Signe watched her. "You know," she remarked, "if you have any trouble solving it, feel free to come and chat. I'm not as good with these things as our friend Lucas, but I do have a little personal history with secret codes." She took off her red glasses, and Zoe could see that her eyes were sparkling.

Zoe waited for Signe to explain, to possibly reveal something about her mysterious past, but she didn't. And perhaps Signe was expecting a follow-up question, maybe she was even inviting Zoe to inquire about her "little personal history." But right then Zoe had something else on her mind.

"Do you know anything about the Mayan glyph?" she asked. "Did they figure it out yet?" She looked Signe right in the eye, just as Mackenzie had advised.

"Yes, I believe they have," Signe replied. "But of course, Mayan writing is not my particular passion. What intrigues me is the process—*how* they arrived at the translation."

She wiped her glasses with her sleeve, and then put them back on.

"Do you remember," she added pleasantly, "I once said to you that any real achievement requires three things: precision, patience, and intuition. Intuition is the most precious, of course, but it's no use until you trust it. But why am I telling you all this, Zoe? You should be telling me."

*Telling her what?* Zoe wondered.

She waited for Signe to speak again. But when Signe just returned to her desk and started shuffling papers around, Zoe picked up her backpack and quietly left the classroom.

# 26

That afternoon Zoe went to the Hubbard library. She found a carrel near the windows and carefully unfurled the little roll of notebook pages. Then she began playing with the crazy symbols, rewriting them, reversing them, trying to detect patterns or keywords. But without Lucas sitting beside her to give her hints, she wasn't getting very far. All she'd figured out was that the word she'd read—"Zoe"—was somehow the number 553415. Six numbers, and there were three letters in her name. So maybe Z=55, O=34, and E=15. But why? What sense did that make? And what could she do with this, anyway?

Then she noticed that a certain sequence of numbers always seemed to appear right next to "Zoe:" 14114211. The second pair of numbers was the same as the fourth. Obviously, this had to be "Dara."

*Oh, joy,* Zoe thought. *So I guess this means I've finally solved Dara Grosbard!* Well, at least she'd gotten three good letters out of her former friend: *D, A,* and *R.* And if she added them to the letters in her own name, she could use the

cipher to encrypt zillions of important words. Like "read."
And "doze." And "daze."

She looked out the window. It was early November,
and the almost-winter afternoon was already turning dark.
Streetlights were coming on, and she could see various
theater-types milling around on the sidewalk in front of
the lobby, rehearsals apparently over for the day. She wondered when the musical was opening. Whenever Isadora
had the lead, Mom would always tape a big gold star on
the refrigerator calendar for Opening Night, so that there
was no chance that anyone in the family would make other
plans. But of course Isadora wasn't in the play this time.
The Bennetts would probably go anyway, to cheer her on
as she assistant stage-managed, but so far the calendar
was empty, and the family hadn't even bought tickets.

Zoe picked up her pencil again, a blue mechanical
pencil she'd lately begun using. "Zore," she wrote in
number-cipher. "Rezo." And then she thought of an actual
word she could make: "zero." That sure seemed fitting:
"Zoe + Dara = zero."

She wrote the equation in cipher: "553415 + 14114211 =
55154234."

But even as she carefully traced the funny math of
Lucas's cipher, she knew she hadn't solved anything.

Because really, after all this time, how could her friendship with Dara equal zero? Zero meant there was nothing between them, and maybe there never had been. But in her heart she knew this wasn't true. The equation was logical, but it wasn't the whole story.

And then she looked up. Someone was pulling a chair over to her carrel. Dara.

"Hey," Dara was saying in a library voice. "Okay if I join you?"

Zoe nodded uncertainly. "Why not."

"Rehearsal just ended, and Mackenzie told me she saw you coming here. So, what are you doing?" Dara glanced blankly at the encrypted "Zoe + Dara" equation.

"It's a cipher," Zoe said, tucking her hair behind her ears. "I'm just kind of messing with it, actually."

"Yeah, I heard you were obsessed with all that."

"You did? Who told you?"

"Signe. She's telling the whole school. She's like your personal publicity department."

Zoe giggled nervously. "Really? That's weird."

"You think so?" Dara shrugged. "You know what's really weird, Zoe? That I never got any of this about you."

Zoe flinched. Was that an accusation? Was she saying

Zoe had kept it from her? Or was she maybe blaming herself for not seeing things better?

"It's not your fault," Zoe said quickly.

"Oh, I'm not saying it is! I'm just saying it's weird. I mean, I always knew you were a little warped, but..."

"Gee, thanks."

Dara gave a short laugh. "Anyway, I just wanted to tell you that I think it's incredibly cool."

"Okay. Well, thank you. I mean it, Dara."

There was an awkward pause, and Zoe thought, *Okay. Now it's my turn to say something about her.* "So when's Opening Night?"

"Friday. I'm incredibly nervous. Leg says—" Dara stopped. "Sorry. You don't want to hear what Leg says, I bet."

Zoe smiled. "It's okay, Dara. Really."

"She says if you're not scared, that's a bad sign."

"She's probably right."

"Yeah. She's not totally stupid, Zoe."

"I never said she was."

Then Dara started chewing her cuticles, and Zoe thought, *Well, maybe I haven't solved Dara after all. Because why is she even here? Is she waiting for something?*

*Okay, talk!* she yelled at herself. *Just do it! Now!*

"Listen, Dara, I'm not really sure what happened with us, but—"

"Don't worry," Dara interrupted. "I'm not even mad at you anymore. About the play *or* Lucas."

"You're not?"

"Well, I still think he's obnoxious. And the notes were definitely psychotic, but at least he admitted he wrote them. Oh, and he apologized to me. Did he tell you that?"

"No, actually. I'm glad he did."

"Anyway," Dara said, sighing. "I wanted to apologize too. I should have talked to you more. About the notes and everything else."

"That's okay," Zoe answered. And then before she had time to choose the perfect words, she said, "Listen, Dara. I'm really, really glad you're in the play. I just didn't understand before how something could be so important to you, and maybe you didn't even know it. And then when you finally figure it out, it kind of shakes you up, and you feel completely different, but also like *yourself*. And you expect everybody to just get it and be happy for you. But how can they, if you never share it, and you always keep everything all locked up—"

"Hey, Zoe, forget it," Dara said gently. "Let's just say we both messed up, okay? Besides, things are better like this.

We needed to make new friends, didn't we?"

"I know." Zoe swallowed. It was true; she understood it now, but that didn't make it easier. "Anyway, I'm incredibly sorry."

Dara widened her big gray-blue eyes. "But maybe we can still hang out sometime? I don't mean like before, but..."

"I'd really like that," Zoe said quickly.

Then Dara grinned. It was the old Dara grin, as easy to read as a traffic sign. Maybe she hadn't totally changed after all, Zoe thought. And maybe the equation had been wrong. Maybe "Zoe + Dara" didn't equal zero. Maybe it equaled three or eleven or thirty-six billion. Or maybe it wasn't even a number. Maybe it was something else entirely, like green.

"Oh, there you are," a voice called. It was Paloma, who was taking big, impatient steps toward them. Zoe could see Leg standing at the circulation desk, talking on her cell phone. "We were downstairs waiting for you. Remember, Dara?"

"Sorry," said Dara. "I was just coming." Suddenly she jumped up. "Gasp," she cried. "I almost forgot!" She unzipped her backpack and handed Zoe a glossy-looking publication. "This just came out," she said hurriedly. "The December issue. Hot off the presses."

Zoe glanced at the cover: the *Hubbard News*. That horrible, braggy magazine Owen kept in his office. "Why are you giving me this?"

"Check out page thirteen."

"So you're ready?" Paloma asked loudly. "Leg has a doctor's appointment. Her mom's waiting."

"I said I'm coming." Dara looked at Zoe. "See you at Opening Night?"

"Of course," Zoe said. But suddenly she remembered something. "I haven't bought a ticket yet."

"That's okay," Dara replied. She rolled her eyes. "My parents bought like twenty extra. I'll give you one."

"Thanks."

"No problem. Well, see you later, Zoe. Wave." And then Dara followed Paloma and Leg out of the library.

Zoe waited for the library doors to close. She sat back down at her carrel, opened the *Hubbard News*, and flipped to page thirteen.

This fall, twelve-year-old **Lucas Joplin** identified an ancient Mayan hieroglyph as part of a writing system centuries older than previously discovered glyphs. The meaning of the glyph has not yet been determined, but archeologists speculate that it might be an early representation of a certain sky god thought to reside simultaneously in all four corners of the earth.

"Lucas's contribution to our understanding of the ancient world may be truly remarkable," Ancient Civilizations teacher Signe Sorenson explains. "But he couldn't have done it without the extraordinary collaboration of Hubbard sixth grader **Zoe Bennett**." Herself a promising cryptanalyst, Zoe is now in her seventh year at the school.

"Four blue," Zoe whispered to herself. "Four blue." She sat there for a moment, feeling her heart race.

Then she ran upstairs to the third floor and banged on Signe's door.

# ANSWER KEY

**Page 29**

The first cipher is a basic substitution cipher—it simply substitutes nonsense letters for the letters of the alphabet, as follows:

| b | g | w | ɱ | H | ɔ | ɾ | ʃ | ɑ | ↄ | ⅄ | k | σ |
|---|---|---|---|---|---|---|---|---|---|---|---|---|
| A | B | C | D | E | F | G | H | I/J | K | L | M | |

| ᴕ | x | ∞ | : | ʁ | ⅃ | ϯ | ɪ | ⊥ | ɱ | ʃ | oɾ | |
|---|---|---|---|---|---|---|---|---|---|---|---|---|
| N | O | P | Q | R | S | T | U/V | W | X | Y | Z | |

Many ciphers are substitution ciphers. This particular one was used by Mary, Queen of Scots, to secretly communicate her plot to overthrow Queen Elizabeth I. When it was deciphered, she was convicted and beheaded for treason.

Lucas has written: *"I hate this stupid place. What am I doing here, wasting my time?"*

The second cipher was invented by the nineteenth-century American writer and poet Edgar Allan Poe. In an essay titled "A Few Words on Secret Writing," he provided this substitution cipher:

| symbol | shall stand for | letter | symbol | " | " | " | letter |
|---|---|---|---|---|---|---|---|
| ) | shall stand for | a | ' | " | " | " | n |
| ( | " " " | b | † | " | " | " | o |
| — | " " " | c | ‡ | " | " | " | p |
| * | " " " | d | ¶ | " | " | " | q |
| . | " " " | e | ☞ | " | " | " | r |
| , | " " " | f | ] | " | " | " | s |
| ; | " " " | g | [ | " | " | " | t |
| : | " " " | h | £ | " | " | " | u or v |
| ? | " " " | i or j | $ | " | " | " | w |
| ! | " " " | k | ¿ | " | " | " | x |
| & | " " " | l | ¡ | " | " | " | y |
| o | " " " | m | ☜ | " | " | " | z |

Translated, Lucas's second message is *"I should be in Guatemala."*

## Pages 43–44

The first part of Lucas's writing is more of the Mary, Queen of Scots cipher. It says: *"The one named Dara just said sigh."*

The second part is a Caesar cipher, used by the Roman emperor Julius Caesar. To fool his enemies, Caesar shifted the Latin alphabet three spaces. Of course, here Lucas is shifting the English alphabet as follows:

| Plain:  | A | B | C | D | E | F | G | H | I |
|---------|---|---|---|---|---|---|---|---|---|
| Cipher: | X | Y | Z | A | B | C | D | E | F |

| Plain:  | J | K | L | M | N | O | P | Q | R |
|---------|---|---|---|---|---|---|---|---|---|
| Cipher: | G | H | I | J | K | L | M | N | O |

| Plain:  | S | T | U | V | W | X | Y | Z |
|---------|---|---|---|---|---|---|---|---|
| Cipher: | P | Q | R | S | T | U | V | W |

Lucas's message reads: *"Leg said blah, blah, blah. I don't like her."*

The third part is based on the Polybius checkerboard, or Greek square, invented by the ancient Greek historian Polybius more than 2,200 years ago. Each letter of the alphabet is represented by two digits according to its place on this checkerboard:

|   | 1 | 2 | 3 | 4   | 5 |
|---|---|---|---|-----|---|
| 1 | A | B | C | D   | E |
| 2 | F | G | H | I/J | K |
| 3 | L | M | N | O   | P |
| 4 | Q | R | S | T   | U |
| 5 | V | W | X | Y   | Z |

For example, the letter *S* is represented by the number 43—4 for the row across, 3 for the column down. *E* is 15, 1 for the column across, 5 for the column down. So the word "see" is enciphered: 431515. The letters *I* and *J* share the number 24—you'll need to figure out which is the right letter.

Here Lucas has written: *"I think the girl named Zoe looks interesting."* He's written Zoe as 553415, but she's read her name without realizing it. She begins to understand how this cipher works in the last chapter, when she figures out her name and also "Dara."

## Page 93

This is the Pigpen cipher, which Lucas explains on page 181. Originating during the Crusades, it was further developed in the eighteenth century by a secret society called the Freemasons. This message reads: *"Hey, Zoe, what does this say?"*

## Pages 158, 174

Pigpen again: *"The gecko never blinks … but Zoe never opens her eyes."*

# SOURCES

**Books About Codes and Ciphers**

Paul B. Janeczko, *Top Secret: A Handbook of Codes, Ciphers, and Secret Writing*, Cambridge, Mass.: Candlewick Press, 2004.

Karin N. Mango, *Codes, Ciphers, and Other Secrets*, New York: Franklin Watts, 1988.

Mark Fowler and Radhi Parekh, *Codes & Ciphers, Usborne Superpuzzles—Advanced Level*, Tulsa, Okla.: EDC Publishing, 1995.

Joel Rothman and Ruthven Tremain, *Secrets with Ciphers and Codes*, New York: Macmillan, 1969.

Simon Singh, *The Code Book*, New York: Anchor Books/ Random House, 1999. This isn't a kid's book and it's hard, but if you're fascinated by codes and ciphers, give it a try!

**Books About Mayan Civilization and Writing**

There are many great books in the adult section of your library. To learn how Mayan scholars try to decipher Mayan writing, read Michael D. Coe's *Breaking the Maya Code*

(New York: Thames and Hudson, 1992). For a more general look at Mayan civilization, try *The World of the Ancient Maya* by John S. Henderson (Ithaca, N.Y.: Cornell University Press, 1981) and *Everyday Life of the Maya* by Ralph Whitlock (New York: Dorset Press, 1987, © 1976). A word of warning, though: The photos in these books are amazing, but the text can be pretty challenging.

Two fun and kid-friendly books are:

Nancy Day, *Your Travel Guide to Ancient Mayan Civilization*, Minneapolis: Runestone Press, 2001.

Elizabeth Baquedano, *Aztec, Inca & Maya*, Eyewitness Books, New York: Alfred A. Knopf, 1993.